INTERLAND

INTERLAND SERIES BOOK #2

GARY CLARK

GCL
BOOKS

For Evan

JAY Toyah Sammy Cassie Pinto STITCH

INTERLAND

PART I

1

The sea made a white streak across the horizon where rolling waves broke on the sandbanks. From the crest of Highdown Hill, one of the three highest points in the county, Cassie stood facing the ocean and kicking at the dirt, sending shards of flint spinning over the ledge. Darkness had drawn in. She hugged her arms to her body and shivered.

Her eyes rested on the Beach Lane Café, visible in silhouette against the light grey sea, its stilts holding it gracefully aloft above the stones. To the north, the dip, slope and soar of hill upon hill felt intimidating, sheer power trapped in land.

Cassie absently scratched at her arm. She glanced at the dark tattoo-like number, seven, distinct against the pale skin of her inner wrist. She couldn't hide her sense of pride. Never would she have believed she could be a level seven. Her power gave her freedom. She was a *Runner*.

The ring of trees decorating the top of Highdown was a distinctive feature of all the hill forts in the south – sacred places for some, popular locations to congregate for others. A small campfire gathered momentum in the centre of the inner ring. Around the fire was a familiar scene: figures huddled for warmth, some sitting, some moving in the night air. Waves of energy flowed from the land. All three of the hill forts in the area attracted their fair share of visitors, including the spiritualists, chanting incantations to ward off the Devil, drinking wine to ward off the cold.

As she watched, Reuben's athletic figure came into view, skirting the ring of trees. He strode with a confidence that both impressed and annoyed Cassie in equal measure. The world seemed to make way for Reuben, to accommodate him. He was born lucky. He was a Runner, like her, but more experienced. He'd been making trips out of the Interland for over three years, whereas this was Cassie's first proper mission, not counting the training excursions with Zadie Lawrence. Those early trips out of the Interland were simply to familiarise Cassie with the requirements of the Runners – the dangers and the importance of keeping out of sight and moving quickly. *Get out, get the mission done, get home.* The Interland was safety.

She noticed Reuben do a double take at the sight of the hooded figures around the fire, heads down as if in prayer. He had a smirk on his face as he approached Cassie. 'Something odd going on over there,' he said.

'Someone has to keep the Devil out,' Cassie said, returning Reuben's smile. Out towards the sea, total darkness approached and Cassie was glad of Reuben's presence. He stood alongside her so that their arms touched, the shiver that moved over her skin reminding Cassie of the strength of feeling that had once existed between them.

Reuben pointed to the west, to the estuary of the River Arun. 'West Beach,' he said. It was the place where Reuben first reached out to Cassie and her close friend, Jay, before they came to the Interland.

'You never stopped to talk,' Cassie said, a bitterness coming through in her tone that she hadn't intended. However much she told herself that she forgave Reuben for leaving when they were young, she'd not forgotten. The Interland had drawn both Reuben and her grandad away from her without warning, and now her grandad was gone. Forever. He died just a few months after their reunion at the Interland. It was as if he'd reached the end of his journey and was happy to leave. She had to relive being abandoned by him all over again. Their reunion had not been long enough for Cassie to get to know him again, but long enough for his loss to hit hard once more.

She had loved Reuben when they were younger. As deeply as she could have imagined back then in her early teens. Now? It was complicated. They'd been apart for too long. So much had passed. She'd changed – turned twenty. Then there was Sammy, Jay's brother. At nearly eighteen, he'd moved from being her best friend's kid brother to something more. Their connection was undeniable. Even thinking of him now made a small heat blossom in her chest, followed quickly by a pang of guilt.

She turned to Reuben. 'So have you figured out the route?' her tone a little warmer than before.

'We can train-hop most of the way. If we hit trouble, we get off and go cross-country on foot.'

Over the past year, the excursions of the Runners had become more dangerous. Rundown districts had enveloped entire towns. Frequent power cuts and empty supermarket shelves meant desperate, fearful people. Then there was the Given. Back before Cassie found the sanctuary of the Interland, before the Zadie Lawrence protest that fuelled the crackdown by the State, the Given walked freely among the public. They enjoyed similar rights and were respected. Now, the Given had been pushed into extinction. The few that remained outside the Interland were in hiding, scared for their lives.

'How far?'

'We'll be there by lunchtime tomorrow. We can bed down here tonight, head off at first light.' Reuben turned, motioning for Cassie to follow back to their camp.

Cassie touched his arm. 'Hey, sorry,' she said.

'What for?' Reuben stopped.

'Just now. Didn't mean to snap.'

'Didn't notice,' Reuben said, turning away.

Cassie watched as he scuffed through the long grass towards the ring of trees, the fire now raging so that the tree trunks flickered orange. She followed in his path. They'd set up camp over the north ledge, out of sight and sheltered from the southerly wind. She caught up with him and linked arms as they passed through the ring of trees, avoiding the inner circle so as not to disturb the pagans. He glanced at her, but something over Cassie's shoulder caught his eye. He stopped. Cassie turned to see the group of pagans stand and push down their hoods as they looked towards the two Runners. Cassie took a step back. 'Can you feel it?' she said.

'Power,' Reuben said. 'Lots of it.'

'They must have been shielding. These aren't pagans,' said Cassie. 'We need to leave.' Before they'd moved more than a few metres, more figures appeared at the outer circle of trees.

'Readers,' said Reuben.

Cassie's heart raced, her mind spinning with questions.

'How did they know we'd be here?' she said as Reuben held tight to her arm.

Two of the figures stepped aside to allow someone through. A man emerged, a silhouette in the shadow of the moon as he approached Cassie and Reuben.

2

At just past noon in the main cavern, the dining hall, beams of light from above reflected off the rocks, bouncing around the cavern as if they were alive. Trailing branches, bracken and ivy snaked through the opening towards the inner sanctum. Birdsong echoed above Jay's head, distracting her from her book. A cool stream of air flowed over her face and she closed her eyes, taking a deep breath. The air was fresh, scented by the woodland above.

'Hey,' said Pinto, approaching and taking a seat next to Jay. Pinto was eight years old. He arrived at the Interland with his sister, Toyah, nearly two years before Jay arrived with friends Cassie and Stitch, and her brother, Sammy.

'Hi you,' said Jay, gazing at her little friend with his smooth complexion, hair down at his shoulders and his deep brown eyes. 'Where have you been, beautiful boy? Health Centre?' As part of his study, Pinto shadowed the doctors.

Pinto ignored Jay's question. 'You seen Toyah?' he asked.

His sister was nearly ten years older, her mark well

defined on the inside of her arm – a level six. They came to the Interland alone, no parents, no explanation. They chose not to tell of their past, and Jay never asked. Most people in the Interland had a difficult story – people they left behind, or people they ran from. Jay shook her head. 'You looked in her room?'

Pinto nodded, then slumped his shoulders. He looked up into the roof of the cavern. 'What were you looking at?'

Jay returned her gaze to the roof. 'Breathing in some of the freedom.'

'The outside?' asked Pinto. 'Toyah says that *inside* is freedom. Where there aren't any Readers. But I'm not sure.'

Jay slung an arm around him and smiled. His face flushed a little. 'Toyah's right,' Jay said. 'The world out there's got worse since I arrived here, and a lot worse since the last time you were out there. You're in the safest place you can be right now.'

'Readers are no bother for you, with your power,' Pinto said.

Jay lowered her gaze. 'It's not always that easy. Can't say I've managed to get a hold on the power yet. And there are some powerful Readers out there.'

Pinto looked Jay in the eye. 'More powerful than you?'

Jay shrugged. 'Who knows? Best we don't find out if you ask me.'

'How do you know how bad it is out there?' Pinto craned his neck to see as high as he could.

'Intelligence from the Runners. Hey, you could be a Runner one day?'

Pinto shrugged. 'Might not have power.'

'You will.' Jay felt Pinto's power already. He'd be strong. Alfred, the bookseller who had helped Jay find the Interland, was convinced Pinto had something special. Not a level eight but something far rarer, a level five in the making. Alfred always had a strong intuition for people's level of power. There were no level five Given inside the Interland or anywhere else as far as Alfred knew. He said that a level five was the only one to have the power over inanimate objects – a telekinetic ability. But they could be unpredictable. Alfred described it as being like an unstable element, its electrons spinning around a central nucleus with an imbalance, liable to break up with great force. So they needed to work hard at controlling their power, harder than most.

Jay sensed Pinto already felt the beginnings of his power. When Jay was his age, she too had felt her power fizzing just below her ability to control it. 'Show me,' she said, reaching for his wrist.

'I'm only eight,' Pinto said.

Jay grabbed for him, tickling him until he squealed. 'Show me,' she said, pulling back his sleeve. 'Oh my word, a level nine,' Jay shouted out. 'Someone come quick, we have a level nine here, help, the power is too much...' Pinto giggled and tried to pull away from Jay. She held him tight, and they laughed.

'Hey,' Jay said. 'Have you looked for Toyah at the Free Cave?' Jay's brother Sammy discovered the Free Cave not long after they'd arrived at the Interland. It was a place they'd kept to themselves. Other than Sammy, Jay and Stitch, only Pinto and Toyah knew of it. To get there, you had to pass through the residential wing and up into an opening in the roof of the passage near Sammy's room. Sammy often explored the tunnels and caves on his own, discovering openings and connections between the different bits of the Interland, including a hidden passage through to the Interland stores he used to sneak food back to his room. One route he followed, eventually wound its way to a spectacular cavern that they all named the *Free Cave*.

'She wouldn't go there on her own,' said Pinto.

'She might be with Sammy?'

Pinto shrugged. Jay nudged into him and jumped up off their rock seat. 'Let's go look.'

* * *

JAY AND PINTO checked Sammy's room on their way to the connection. It was empty. The opening in the cave roof just past Sammy's room, in the dead-end section of tunnel, was virtually invisible in the darkness.

'Come on,' said Pinto, nodding up at the ceiling.

Jay looked back down the tunnel, then to Pinto. 'You sure you're up for this?'

Pinto rolled his eyes and gestured for Jay to help him up. She linked her hands together to form a foothold for Pinto and he launched himself towards the opening, holding Jay's shoulders and squeezing through the hole. Jay jumped and edged her elbows over the ledge, pulling herself up with help from Pinto. Pinto twisted the end of his torch, focusing it to a wide angle. He scurried ahead, crouching below the low ceiling. Even in the light of the torch, the walls were black as coal.

'Slow down,' called Jay. 'Remember the drop.'

After just a few minutes, as Jay's back began to ache from bending over, they approached the first drop. Sammy had reached this point three times and headed back before his fourth visit, when he decided to lower himself over the edge. The shaft curves, so a torch only illuminates about halfway down the fifty-foot drop. But it's not far before the shaft levels out to a steeply sloping tunnel and then to horizontal again. It's easy when you know this, but Jay wondered some-times about her brother, and how he took that leap of faith the first time.

Pinto didn't hesitate. He turned around and grinned at Jay as he lowered himself backwards into the hole, his torch clutched between his teeth. Jay let him get some distance and then followed, catching him up as he paused for breath at the bottom of the shaft. 'This is the best bit.' He nodded ahead.

The passageway opened out so they could easily stand. They picked up speed, Pinto breaking into a run as light entered the tunnel through cracks in the rocks. Through the smaller cracks, water seeped into their pathway, like a series of little waterfalls that Pinto dashed through, laughing and skipping at every one. The combination of the light through the rocks and the water gave a sense of the unreal. Jay felt that in this place was the true magic and wonder of the Interland.

They reached the junction. Sammy called it the *fifty-fifty* place, joking that if you took the wrong branch, then that would be the last you would see of the world. He said the wrong branch led deep into the earth where light could not penetrate, and where all life was sucked into the walls of the tunnels and nothing could survive. Jay smiled at the thought of Sammy's embellishments, much like their dad used to do when he read them stories as kids.

'Left,' said Pinto.

Jay laughed, 'Sure, you go left and see who gets there first.'

Pinto grinned and bolted through the opening to the right branch. Jay thought about her friend, Stitch. He hated the tunnels. Any hole narrower than he was tall would be too much of a psychological barrier for Stitch. He'd only been to the Free Cave once and spent the entire time fretting that he wouldn't be able to get back and that he'd have to live out his days trapped in the irony of the Free Cave.

Jay and Stitch had drifted apart since being inside the Interland, despite the strength of the connection of their power. The closer the energy connected them, the further apart Jay felt. Stitch was preoccupied with the technicalities of the power, how it worked, and how they should channel it. Jay could become absorbed in the feelings, the sense of the energy, but not so much in the physics of what was going on, as was Stitch's distraction. Jay missed him.

In the tunnels, Cassie was the opposite of Stitch. Jay was certain that Cassie had been to the Free Cave more than any of the rest of them, even Sammy, and probably she'd been further. If there was somewhere difficult to reach, Cassie would be the one to give it a go.

'What are you frowning at?' said Pinto, interrupting Jay's thoughts.

Jay smiled. 'Just thinking about Cassie.'

'She's the best Runner. The toughest,' said Pinto.

'She is,' Jay said as they reached their next and penultimate obstacle before the Free Cave. She stopped at the edge of a drop that reminded her of the water slide at the pool back home. Except this one had no guarantees of a soft landing. Jay hesitated, peering down the steep slope.

'Scared?' Pinto smiled. To answer her little challenger, Jay stepped over the edge, crouching and using her feet to slide down the water-smoothed slope and into the darkness. Just past the first bend, the slope steepened and Jay knew she'd have to lean back and slide on her backside if she was to avoid tipping forward and launching herself head-first. Her heart raced. Even after a dozen times, her stomach floated through her chest to her throat and she let out a scream. Pinto laughed as he piled into her from behind and they both rolled down the final few feet towards the cave.

* * *

JAY AND PINTO stepped into the Free Cave at a ledge around ten feet from the ground. Light pushed in through the roof where tree roots had grown through the rock, opening up the ceiling in great sections and proving the strength of flora over rock. Boulders the size of London black cabs had fallen from the roof and nestled in the ground below them, carpeted in a deep green moss. The nearest boulder was close enough for Jay to jump to, then the next led her and Pinto to the floor of the cavern. They stopped, and Pinto pointed. 'There,' he said. Sammy and Toyah had climbed the east rock face and reached the high ledge. Sammy always said that the high ledge was a potential alternative route out of the Free Cave, and would be the next stage of his exploration. Cassie declared that she would be first to get up there and see where it led, but it seemed Sammy and Toyah had beaten her to it.

Sammy reached for Toyah's hand and Jay glanced at Pinto, but his attention was on the ground – searching for interesting stones. Sammy and Toyah held hands as they moved forward into the cave together.

'Toyah,' called Pinto as he reached the base of the cliff, looking for a place to climb.

Toyah and Sammy emerged from the cave once more, and Toyah called for her brother to stay put. 'We will come back down.'

Jay found a rock to rest on as Pinto scurried around, occasionally leaning down to pick up a stone, examining it for a moment before putting it in his pocket or throwing it into a pool of water. Jay closed her eyes, enjoying the deep connection she felt with the earth. A warm glow seeped into the back of her eyes and the sounds of the cavern were drowned by the whispers – soft at first, then more urgent, merging to a white noise. The white glow intensified, and she was dizzy, her head swimming with the force of the power.

'Jay.' Her brother's voice, his hands on her shoulders, gently shaking her. The whispers dissipated, the glow subsided, and she opened her eyes. 'You having one of your moments?' he smiled.

'I'm OK,' said Jay.

She looked up to see Pinto jostling with Toyah. Toyah said: 'You know you're not supposed to come down here without me.'

'But...'

'But, nothing. With me or not at all. OK?'

Jay turned back to Sammy. 'Hey,' she said. 'You made it up there.' She nodded towards the high ledge.

'Piece of cake.'

'Does it lead anywhere?'

'Somewhere. But we didn't get far. Just into the entrance there, then it tightens up, too small to walk through.'

Jay looked over at Toyah, then back to Sammy with a smile. He shrugged, non-committal, and Jay decided not to ask.

'Cassie back yet?' Sammy asked.

'Not yet.' Jay sensed something was wrong but couldn't get the feeling into focus. She looked at Sammy for confirmation of her gut feeling. 'Do you sense anything?'

Sammy shook his head. 'I'm sure she'll be fine.'

* * *

JAY WOKE FROM A RECURRING NIGHTMARE, her body covered in sweat. She blindly scrabbled in the dark to get a hold on something. The clutter on her bedside shelf clattered to the floor. She tried to slow her racing thoughts – to understand where she was. That space between dream and reality terrified Jay – that moment in which it was impossible to be sure whether the images imprinted on her mind were real, or if they were part of a dream.

The nightmares were always the same. She was in the cavern. Marcus was there, the leader and most powerful of the State's Readers. She re-lived the moment he and the Readers closed in. The events of that day merged and twisted together in her nightmares. The pain that he caused when he infiltrated her mind was amplified in her dreams, and she couldn't shake him out of her head. Sammy's injuries were so bad, and she couldn't reach him. Stitch was gone. She called for him, but he never responded.

Every time, she woke with tears streaming down her face, sweat pouring off her body, and hyperventilating so much that she would see stars.

She stood, straining to catch a glimpse of light from the rocks above but getting nothing but darkness. She felt around the floor of her room for her torch. Her hand closed around its cold metal and she breathed a sigh of relief as the light bounced around her room, bringing her back to her real world, the one in which Marcus was no longer a threat.

The man stood in the shadow of a tree so that Cassie couldn't see his face. She looked him up and down. He was no taller than her. No power that she could sense. It was true that, unless the shielding was expert, she'd be able to sense power in someone this close. 'Who are you? What do you want?'

'Call me Hinton,' he said, his voice calm and measured, then flicked his head to signal for the Readers to back off. They melted into the background, just a handful remaining within earshot.

The uneasy feeling in Cassie's stomach radiated to her skin. 'We'll be off then,' she said, stepping back.

'Stay. Show me your mark,' Hinton said, quiet but firm. A Reader approached Cassie and before she registered his movement had taken her by her left hand and roughly pulled back her sleeve. Hinton glanced at her number —seven.

Reuben stepped forward, raising a hand, but before he made contact with the Reader, he doubled over in pain, clutching the sides of his head, screaming like a trapped animal. Three more Readers approached and focused on Reuben, Hinton remaining in the shadows. Cassie could feel their energy piling into her friend. Instinctively, she stood between Reuben and the Readers, trying to deflect their attack.

Hinton raised a hand, and his soldiers stopped their digging. Reuben collapsed onto the floor. Cassie knelt next to him and witnessed a scar form on the right side of his face, a scar characteristic of the effects of Reader attacks on the mind – a scar like the one displayed by Zadie Lawrence back at the Interland. Reuben's eyes swam with a mist of confusion as he slumped onto his side, curling tighter into a ball with every laboured breath.

'What do you want?' Cassie snarled at Hinton. 'Show me your face.'

'You're Cassie,' the man said.

'Congratulations,' said Cassie, trying not to reveal her uneasiness about him knowing her name. Hinton laughed without humour, then gave an almost imperceptible flick of his head to his Readers. Cassie felt a sharp pain enter both sides of her head at her temples, a pain so intense that her legs almost buckled. She swayed, her hands to her head, eyes streaming. As suddenly as it had begun, the pain seeped away, leaving her reeling.

The man waved back his Readers once more. So he had no direct power of his own. He was not one of the Given. But he had something more powerful – he had control. The Readers moved quickly, responded to his signals as if it were the man himself inflicting the attacks. And, more than that, he had a resistance. Cassie could not read him.

Reuben's eyes remained closed, his breathing shallow. The scar on the side of his face had taken the shape of a long curve from temple to chin and he was trembling, barely conscious.

'Let's go,' said Hinton, turning, instructing Cassie to follow. She stood firm, glancing down at her friend and back to Hinton. 'Oh, the boy? You don't think we should leave him here?' Cassie remained silent, trying again to read the man but getting nothing. A flicker of annoyance emanated from Hinton's dark outline, coming through in his voice. 'Come with me. Now, or you join your friend.'

Cassie knelt next to Reuben, stroked his head. The scar had reddened, almost glowing in the darkness. She took a deep breath, held it. Tensed her muscles and sprang.

Hinton barely had to move to avoid the impact of Cassie. Once more, pain coursed through Cassie's head, her neck and shoulders. Through blurred vision, she saw Hinton's face emerge from shadow as he watched her suffer the pain. She hit the ground, a face full of the wood-land floor at the man's feet. She shrivelled like a burning leaf, tightening. She screamed but heard nothing. Flopped further to the floor, the pain receding, Cassie prised her eyes open a crack. Three men in dark clothes stood over her. Hinton walked away. The Readers leaned close to Reuben, and he writhed in pain once more, but he made no attempt to get away, or even to lift his hands to his head.

'Reuben?' Cassie whispered into the cool, damp air. His body twitched under the focus of the Readers. She tried again to move, but her limbs would not respond, her head like a rock. Hinton glanced at her, then back to Reuben, who had flopped over onto his side so that he faced Cassie, eyes half open with nothing behind. Nothing left. The scar on the side of his face had opened, a crack from which his life seeped.

She looked into his vacant eyes and knew. Reuben was dead.

4

The dining hall cavern bustled with activity. The children laid plates, bowls and cutlery as the day's cooks brought out serving bowls of steaming soup. A well of light penetrated from above, where interconnected caves and channels meandered to the outside world.

Jay scanned the seats around the table for Stitch. He was sat alone, in a world of his own, studying the inside of his wrist. His lop-sided hair had grown so that his fringe covered one eye. She tapped him on the shoulder and slumped down on the bench next to him, making him jump. Jay laughed, 'Looking for something new?' He motioned to his wrist where the letter "C" was displayed in pitch black.

He pulled his sleeve back further. 'I'm the only one in this place without a number,' he said, flicking his hair out of his eyes.

'You're special, like you always said.' Jay nudged into him, then reached to tear some bread from the homemade loaf in the middle of the table.

'Show me yours again,' said Stitch. Jay sighed and pulled

her own sleeve back to show Stitch the "8C" on her wrist. He leaned in to study it. 'My letter is bigger than yours.'

Jay returned to her food. 'Size isn't everything.' Stitch went back to studying his own wrist. 'What's the problem, Stitch? We've been through this. You have something different to the others, and so do I. You and I are connected. We come as a pair. The same as Sasha Colden.'

'What for?' said Stitch. 'What's the point?'

'Why does there always need to be a point?' Jay knew Stitch felt the intensity of the power they had together. She could feel it herself, even if she didn't always understand it. When she was with him, her inner power took on a different form, something deeper. She felt part of him, like they could be one person. And there was something more: a connection between them and everything around them, from the ground beneath their feet, the air around them, and the water flowing between the rocks.

Stitch shrugged and reached for the bread. 'It scares me. It's big. And it doesn't always add up.'

'I know, but we're safe here. No Reader can get to us here, with the protection of the energy in this place. You feel that?'

A boy ran into the dining hall, panting and stuttering, visibly distressed. Zadie Lawrence crouched next to the boy and held his hands. He took a breath and could eventually get his words out: 'The Runners. Two of them haven't returned. Something must have happened.'

Runners never returned late unless something had happened to stop them returning to the Interland. Jay stood. She knew it was Cassie and Reuben. Even before the boy had spoken, she had a sense something was wrong, that Cassie was either too far away for her to feel her presence, or that something had happened. Stitch looked up at Jay. 'Cassie?'

Jay nodded. She could sense Cassie from a distance. Reuben was not so easy. The strength of connection over distance was as much to do with how well people were connected personally, as it was a product of the strength of their power – their marking. She moved around the table to join Zadie. 'It's Cassie,' Jay said, 'and Reuben.'

'I feel it too,' said Zadie, her expression grave.

Stitch joined them. 'We don't know for sure,' he said.

'It's Cassie. I can feel it,' said Jay.

Stitch shook his head. 'She'll be alright, she's badass. No one messes with Cassie.'

But Zadie looked troubled. There had been more incidents between Runners and Readers recently. The Readers had been increasing their activity, like they were building up to something. Cassie was a high value target. She and Reuben had great power, like all the Runners.

Stitch scratched his head, his frown deepening. 'We need to find them.'

Jay shook her head. 'We can't go out there. Away from the source, we won't have the same strength of power. It's too dangerous.'

'How do you know?' said Stitch, frustration in his voice. 'We've never been out, not since the day we found this place, and our powers were revealed.' He pulled his sleeve back again to display his marking.

'I just know,' Jay said.

'I think Stitch is right, Jay,' said Zadie. 'Someone needs to go after Cassie and it makes sense for it to be you. We can send someone with you.'

'I'll go,' said Stitch.

'No,' said Zadie. 'We need you here to keep a line of communication open with Jay. We can send a Runner.'

'But we're stronger together,' Stitch said.

Zadie ignored him.

Jay sat down on a stool. She tried to push her fears to the back of her mind, the prospect of once more being alone and open to attack from Readers, away from her dad and from Sammy. 'I can't go,' she said, looking up at Stitch, her eyes blurring with the tears forming. 'I'm sorry.'

Stitch nodded.

Zadie sighed, 'We'll work something out.'

5

H inton woke to the sound of screams.

Downstairs, his three-year-old daughter, Megan, squealed with laughter as she was tickled by Sarah, his wife. He smiled and turned onto his side to check the clock. Seven-thirty. If he got up now, he'd have time for a lazy breakfast with his two favourite girls. He slung his legs out of bed and rubbed his eyes in the glare of the light coming through a gap in the curtains. He must fix those curtains. They hung off the end of the runner, several curtain hooks missing.

Megan ran past the foot of the stairs, hysterical with delight. She was closely pursued by Sarah, who caught sight of Hinton as he descended the double-width wooden staircase, dressed ready for work, his tie loose around his neck and his collar up. 'Morning lazy bones,' she said, her smile as bright as the open-plan ground floor where morning sun poured in through a wall of glass.

'Daddy...' came Megan's voice as she hurtled back towards the stairs. Hinton leaned down and whisked her into his arms. He planted a stubbly kiss on her cheek and she recoiled. 'Shave your beard, it's prickly,' she said as she stroked his chin, trying to pull at the hairs.

Sarah headed back towards the kitchen. 'What's today got in store for you?' she asked as she poured coffee for Hinton and topped up her own mug.

Hinton set Megan down and she scuttled off calling for the dog, Misty. 'It'll be busy, some new inmates. I might be late.'

'Can't the others deal with it? Does it always have to be you?'

Hinton gave his wife a look that told her he had no choice. She dropped the subject and handed him his coffee. 'You want eggs?'

'Thanks.' Hinton joined his daughter at the breakfast table, collecting his briefcase on the way and pulling out a file he'd brought home from work.

'What's that,' Megan asked, not taking her eyes off the Lego tower she was constructing on the table.

'Work,' he said.

'Criminmals... crinimals?' Megan asked, struggling with the word.

Hinton laughed, 'I guess.'

'Are all your work friends bad people?'

'No.' Hinton smiled, watching for a moment as Megan carefully placed another Lego brick on the top of her precarious looking tower. 'My work friends are good people. It's the people that we keep there that need guidance.'

'You keep bad people?'

'We look after them, try to help them make good choices.'

'Mummy said I make good choices. Mummy said you help people. I want to help people too.'

'You will, one day.' Hinton closed his file as Sarah placed

two plates of eggs on toast on the table. 'Come on you two,' she said as Megan's Lego tower finally toppled. She giggled as the pieces scattered across the table and onto the floor. Then she crossed her arms and sat back in her seat with her arms folded, a broad grin on her face.

'Butter wouldn't melt,' Hinton said, smiling at his wife.

* * *

CASSIE WOKE, the side of her body numb against the cold floor. The room was mostly shadows, lit only by a single lightbulb recessed into the ceiling. The floor was a solid, smooth metal, and the walls a heavy steel. She raised herself onto her elbows and looked towards the heavy-set metal door. No handle on the inside. No window, nothing.

Her head was a symphony of pain, a dull ache punctuated by crescendos of agony. She struggled to stand, one hand holding her forehead, moving slowly towards the door. She tried to prise it open from the inside. It wouldn't budge. She banged on the wall with her fist, but the steel structure resisted her blows, soaked up the sound as if they were six feet thick.

She thought of Reuben, the blankness in his eyes as the life withdrew from his body. She had watched him slip away, had felt his heartbeat slow, weaken, and then stop. Her own heart ached with the thought. She couldn't believe that he was gone, so soon after they'd got to know each other again. She never told him how much he meant to her.

The door gave a deep clunk and swung inward like the opening to a vault. A man entered and Cassie recognised him from the darkness up on Highdown. She stepped back to put as much distance between them as the cell would allow. His expression was neutral – no hint of interest in her, no urgency. She tried to read behind the expression but got nothing. The door closed with a thump. He stared at Cassie for a moment as he leaned back against the opposite wall, licked his finger and rubbed at an invisible mark on the sleeve of his jacket. He cleared his throat.

'Do you know where you are?'

Cassie shook her head.

Hinton leaned down and brushed at his trouser leg, then stood, pushing himself off the wall and stepping a little closer to Cassie. 'We call it *Education*. The second step in the process, before our customers move on to the final stage of true rehabilitation, where the powers no longer cause them any problems.'

'What *customers*? Prisoners?'

'We don't look at it like that. We think of it more as customers who don't yet know what they are shopping for until they've been through the programme.'

'Well, I can see how that thinking might help you sleep better at night,' Cassie said, her pulse quickening. She was in the prison. She thought of Ben, Jay's dad. Ben had been interned here, a prison for the Given, before escaping to the Interland. He had told her about the place, its three stages: Incarceration, Education and Rehabilitation. No one was ever seen again after moving into *Education* or *Rehabilitation*.

She looked to the door, then to Hinton, a smirk on his face as he returned her gaze. He had no power. There were no Readers in the room. Cassie focused in on the man, his mind, channelling her energy into him, digging.

A sharp pain pierced Cassie's head, and she reeled, slamming back against the solid steel wall before her legs weakened and she couldn't stop herself slumping to a crouch position. She looked around. The man had not moved, but for a widening grin. She stood, refocussed, and dug deeper this time. She could overcome this man; he had no power she could sense. This time the pain took away all the strength in her legs and she collapsed to the floor, panting.

'That won't work in here, Cassie. Look around you.' Hinton motioned around the oppressive, grey cell. 'Nothing living. No natural materials, no windows, no natural light...'

Pain radiated from inside the middle of Cassie's skull. She held her head in her hands as though it might split into pieces. He stepped towards her and crouched. 'You may be having trouble thinking right now, so let me speak clearly: In here, you're mine.' Cassie could feel his breath, fresh with the smell of toothpaste. His clothes exuded a scent of clean washing. He was immaculate.

'Why?' Cassie managed to mumble.

'You'll find out. For now, I'm happy we've managed to do this little experiment with the power of a Runner. That's what they call you, isn't it? A big old level seven like you?' Hinton leaned in and edged back Cassie's sleeve to reveal her number. 'A Runner,' he said, standing to leave. 'You must be so proud. Your pal, Jay, must be really worried about you.'

Cassie startled at his mention of Jay, at the thought that Jay could be a target.

He smiled. 'Oh yes, I know all about your little Interland gang. And you're going to help me find them. They're destined to be my most satisfied customers yet!'

6

I n Jay's room, Sammy and Stitch sat on the bed, Jay on the chair at her little desk fashioned out of the rock. On the chessboard between the two boys, Sammy moved his bishop three squares. 'Check,' he said, then turned back to his sister. 'Anything? Any clues?'

Jay continued to study the map; Sammy shifted between sitting on the bed and standing next to Jay, unable to keep still. 'Chill out, Sammy, let me think.'

Stitch frowned. 'I thought those moved sideways?'

Sammy snorted, 'The rook moves sideways, the bishop diagonally.' Stitch let out a sigh of frustration.

Jay kept bent over the map. 'Highdown,' she said under her breath.

'What about it?' Sammy said as Stitch studied the chessboard.

'If there's somewhere Cassie and Reuben could have run into a Reader, it would be up on one of the hill forts,' said Jay.

'A Reader wouldn't be any bother for Cassie and Reuben. Even for Cassie on her own,' said Sammy.

'Well, something's happened, we know that.'

'We won't know what, unless we head out there and find them,' said Stitch. Zadie wanted Jay to go with another Runner, Davey, to look for Cassie, and for Stitch to stay behind, but Jay had no intention of leaving the safety of the Interland without Stitch.

Sammy paced the room. He nudged Stitch to hurry up with his move. 'Come on. Use your mighty level-C power to get in my head,' Sammy teased.

'Better a level C than nothing,' Stitch said.

Jay looked up at her little brother. 'Anything coming through yet, Sammy?'

Sammy pulled back his sleeve. 'Something, but it could be anything. Probably a level eight.'

'Level zero more like,' said Stitch.

At that moment, Jay's dad came into the room with his friend, Matchstick, and Zadie just behind. Sammy stood. 'Any news?'

'Nothing yet,' said Zadie. 'We've come to speak with Jay.'

Jay looked up from the map. 'They could have run into trouble at Highdown, send the Runners there,' she said.

Zadie looked to Sammy. 'Can you boys leave us for a moment?'

'They can stay,' said Jay. Matchstick sat with Sammy and Stitch.

Zadie gave a shrug and stood next to Jay. 'I want you to reconsider.'

'I'm not going out there,' Jay said, looking to her dad for support.

Ben crouched next to her. 'Jay, we think it's the only way. You're the only one who can track them. No one else here will have the sensitivity, the power.'

'What about her?' Jay nodded at Zadie. 'Or the Runners? Davey can track.'

'I need to stay here,' said Zadie. 'You know that. The people here are my responsibility. But you're right about Davey. He will accompany you. Davey is one of the most experienced Runners. He'll be there to help protect you, and to track Cassie and Reuben.'

'I'll go,' said Sammy.

'No,' Ben said without hesitation. 'You're staying here.'

Jay scowled at her dad. 'So he stays and I go. Why am I the expendable one?'

'Jay,' Ben said. 'That's not it. There's no point in Sammy being exposed again, you know what happened last time. We nearly lost him.'

'I can go,' said Matchstick.

Ben raised his eyebrows at his friend. 'If it needed an old man, then I'd go.'

Jay said, 'Sasha Colden barely left this place once she'd settled here. There was a reason for that. *You* might not get it but I can feel it. If I leave here, especially without my connection, then I'm vulnerable. She was your mum,' Jay said, looking at her dad. 'She was our blood. She knew. Can't you sense it?'

Zadie turned to leave. 'This conversation is over. I'll ask Davey to collect you first thing in the morning, get yourself ready.'

With Zadie gone, Ben stood. He briefly touched Jay's shoulder, then turned to leave. 'It's the only way,' he said, then he and Matchstick left the room.

Jay's mind raced; she took short, shallow breaths. The Readers all around her. She gasped to get a lungful. *It's not real. It's a memory. See the memory. Notice the memory. Sit with the feeling. Feelings can't hurt you.* The Readers closed in. Her breaths shortened as she struggled to squeeze air into her lungs. *Deep breath. In for three... out for four.*

'Easy...' said Stitch, holding out a hand to comfort Jay.

'I've got a bad feeling,' said Jay, brushing him off. 'Something's wrong about all this. We don't know what it's like out there. It's a different place. I'm not a Runner, I don't have what Cassie has. I can't face those Readers again, not like before...' She broke off, sat on her bed with her head in her hands.

Sammy went to her. 'You've changed too, Sis. You're stronger, more powerful than before, and you know more about the power. There's no Reader more powerful than you.'

'What about Marcus?'

'He's dead,' said Sammy.

Jay wasn't so sure. There was never a body, no evidence that he'd gone. It was true that Jay felt nothing of him, but she couldn't be sure.

'Look, Jay. Cassie's up against it right now,' said Sammy. 'You're our best hope to find her and bring her back safely.'

'She means a lot to you, doesn't she?'

'Well, I mean I guess...'

'More than me?'

'Of course not! You're my sister. But maybe I believe in your powers more than you do.'

Stitch sat on the other side of Jay and put a hand on her arm, quickly removing it when Jay flinched. She moved to get away from them, their sympathy and their infuriating encouragement. 'Leave me alone for a bit,' she said. Sammy began to say something but Jay cut him off. 'Now, Sammy. Please.'

The boys filed from Jay's room, Stitch turning as he

reached the door. 'I'll come back later,' he said, then stepped out into the passageway.

Alone, Jay allowed her tears to come, silently forming in the corners of her eyes and running down her face. She rubbed at her cheeks as if trying to scrub away her weakness and fear. 'Why are you so frickin weak? This is Cassie you're talking about. Your friend,' she said under her breath. Then louder, 'Stupid... stupid... stupid,' her voice rising to a scream, which she muffled by lying face down on her bed.

7

Of the three hill forts, Marcus preferred Cissbury, where energy flowed through the layers of history from as far back as 500BC, making its way through the chalk bedrock and flint seams, radiating from the inner circle.

Back when he was a Reader, Marcus drew no power from the hill forts. His power came from the State. That was before his encounter with Jay. She drained him, reduced him, then disappeared into the Interland.

Jay's attack reversed the process of transformation to a Reader that he underwent when he was a young student, the process that took his Given power and elevated him to a Level 8 Reader. Now, once again, he drew power from the environment, as did the rest of the Given. The mark on his wrist was now a smudge.

Since that day, when he clashed with Jay, Marcus had opted out. He could no longer exist in normal society. He was neither a Reader, nor accepted as one of the Given. In a world where wielding the powers of the Given had become a greater crime than any other, Marcus chose anonymity and isolation. And slowly, on his own, the little power he did have grew as he spent time soaking up the energy of the Downs.

On the north side of the Ring, two hundred feet down the slope from the summit, Marcus woke to the sound of birds. Morning light barely penetrated the undergrowth to his den, his home for the most part of twelve months. He shuffled to ease himself out of his cocoon, the tangle of branches, rock and soft woodland materials he had used to fashion a bed, and sat up. He stroked the side of his face, the skin tingling where the two scars extended from his temple down the side of his face, like parallel train tracks curving under as they reached his chin. The first was old, inflicted during his original transformation from the Given to a Reader. It had turned white over the years and hard to the touch. The second was inflicted by the girl, Jay. It was no more than a year old, still red, angry, softer to the touch and sometimes painful – a frequent reminder.

He stood, remaining under cover of bushes and trees in the deep trench that had become his home. It had been built during the War to protect the summit from attack, an anti-tank initiative that now provided Marcus with his own kind of protection. It was somewhere to lose himself, to be alone. He replenished his fire with the driest of the wood from his store, smoke rising almost as soon as the sticks hit the ashes, still hot from the previous night.

A sound caught his attention. He opened up a little, something he avoided for the most part, preferring to remain undetectable, and not least because channelling the power seemed to become more painful as the months passed. A whistle. A man walking his dog on the north face of the hill, closer to Marcus's camp than most ever came. Marcus sensed the man as he continued past with his dog and away to the west. His heart slowed once more to a normal rate, and the experience, the anxiety, put the girl back into his mind – Jay.

He pushed her away and sat by the fire, feeding it with wood and rubbing his hands together to revive feeling in his fingers. The grey monochrome sky was heavy, like a blanket. It was not yet light enough for him to head out on his daily foraging. He preferred not to use his power to hunt, the pain not worth the meagre rewards.

A stag beetle caught his eye, stumbling blindly across the dirt floor towards his boots, the flicker of the flames reflected in the gloss-black shell on its back. He leaned over and moved a stick from its path so that it had a direct passage to his left boot, where it stopped. Its feelers scanned Marcus's scraggy shoe before it mounted and climbed up to settle on his laces, where it decided to rest awhile. Marcus caught himself smiling, an unfamiliar sensation that evaporated as soon as he was conscious of it. He looked into the flames and felt something, like a crack in the curtain of confusion in his mind – there was a fresh wave of activity somewhere, change was coming in on the breeze.

8
_____

J ay lay on her back beneath her blankets, the room
pitch black and her eyes wide open.

When the first light peeked through the crevice
in the rocks above her head, Jay pulled back her
covers and climbed, fully clothed, from her bed. She paced
the room, muttering to herself. 'I can feel it,' she said. There
was an undeniable pull to the source, the epicentre of the
Interland. It promised answers, guidance. With the energy
would come clarity. 'No,' she shouted, stopping still in her
room and staring at the rock wall. *There are no answers in the
source*, she said to herself. *The source has done nothing for me.*

Jay had avoided the depths of the Interland since the last
time she was there, when she had been overcome by the
power. Zadie Lawrence didn't like Jay being there too much.
More frequent visits, Zadie said, could push her too far into
the energy. It could be dangerous if she was not ready. She
needed to take it a step at a time, to try to learn the language
in the whispers from the land, the sea, and the earth.

But of course, she didn't listen. The last time, when she
and Stitch connected with the source, the power was like an

electric bolt. Stitch was thrown clear, but Jay remained connected. It transported her *into* the energy with such force that eventually she passed out. Her memory of the ordeal was weak. It had taken her days just to recover enough to leave her bed.

Now, she needed the source. She descended the six levels into the heart of the underground. Cool air washed over her as she reached the lowest level. She fumbled in the dark for the candle in an alcove at the entrance. Her fingers found the matches, light flickering into the rock-walled room. She lit more candles, set into alcoves in the wall, then turned to the central pillar where water trickled down from above.

Three separate streams – from the Arun, the Rother, and the unnamed river – combined at the centre of a naturally formed column and out in a single flow into the rocks below. Jay reached out her hand and allowed the water of the unnamed river to flow through her fingers, where it seemed to sparkle in the light before merging with the other streams. Her heart pounded. Images of Readers floated through her mind. The energy was strong. In the heart of the Interland she was joined with her history, her grand-mother, Sasha Colden.

She felt a familiar energy. Stitch appeared, looking as if he'd just woken up. 'I knew you were down here,' he said. 'I always know when you are in this place.' He looked around the room, his eyes red in the light from the candles, dark rings around them. 'What are you doing?'

'Looking for inspiration,' said Jay. 'I can feel something.'

Stitch held out a hand to Jay.

'Not now,' she said.

'Just for a moment,' said Stitch, motioning towards the source.

Jay took his extended hand. They locked eyes for a moment, then turned to the source. Together, they pushed their free hands into the pool of water formed from the three separate streams. Jay immediately connected. The whispers came, slow and incoherent at first, great swooping waves of white noise. Then faster, with a familiar urgency. Jay looked to Stitch. His eyes were closed. She turned back to look into the water and began to filter the sounds in her head, to order and interpret them. Shapes and colours emerged from the whispers, shapes bound by feelings and intuition. She sensed a fear within the noise, Cassie's fear, but behind it a greater fear, a fear that threatened them all.

Jay broke the chain, stumbled backwards towards the wall of the cave and crouched on her haunches. Stitch gulped in air. 'Did you feel that?' he said. She staggered towards the entrance to the cave and crawled up the first few steps on her hands and knees as she regained her balance. Stitch called after her, but all she could think of was to get out of the room, to get away from the power of the source, to somewhere she could breathe again.

* * *

BACK IN STITCH'S ROOM, Jay watched as Stitch gathered supplies together in a rucksack. 'What are you doing?' she asked.

Stitch shrugged. 'Whether you like it or not, Zadie is coming for you in a couple of hours with Davey. Better we go now, on our terms.'

'We're leaving?' Jay's heart pounded with fear at the thought of it.

Stitch stared at her. 'You *know* we have to leave.'

'You're coming?'

'Can't let you go without all your weapons,' Stitch said, puffing himself up. 'You need your full power, and you won't get that from Davey.'

Jay helped Stitch squeeze his supplies into his bag – a change of clothes, some food, all protected in plastic bags to keep them dry and protected from the water they would have to negotiate on their way out.

'Are we doing the right thing?' said Jay, her fears lingering.

'Something's happening, and Cassie is in trouble, so we need to go.' Light filled Stitch's room from above. His room was nearer the surface than Jay's, and the routes through to the open air were much bigger, so it was colder, but also much lighter during the day. Stitch finished packing and slung his rucksack onto his back. Jay stood, and together they stopped by Jay's room for her to gather her things, then pushed on to the main hall. Jay's nerves tingled at the prospect of leaving the Interland and once again stepping outside.

The main hall was empty, as they had expected. They continued through to the entry passage, through the waterfall and on to the place where the boulder covered the entrance. Stitch picked up the heavy branch intended as a lever and put his weight on it, shifting the boulder a few feet, enough for Jay to squeeze through the gap and hold it in place for Stitch. When Stitch was through, Jay allowed the boulder to roll back, blocking the light from the Interland and sealing them on the outside.

9

D avey followed Zadie closely through the passageways of the residential section, towards Jay's room. He had been waiting for this. If Davey wanted to fulfil his potential in the Interland, this mission with Jay to find the Readers was his chance. He could prove himself by showing his loyalty to Zadie and to the cause.

Zadie whipped the covers off Jay's bed in exasperation, then turned to scan the room as if Jay could hide in plain sight.

'Where is she?' asked Davey.

Zadie stormed from the room, picking up pace as she headed back into the warren of rock tunnel passageways. She strode into Stitch's room, letting out a groan before sitting down on his bed, her head in her hands.

'What now?' said Davey.

Zadie was silent for a moment, then sprung from the bed. 'You can track, can't you?'

Davey nodded. He was one of the best trackers amongst the Runners. He had a skill for locking on to a single source of energy. 'Those two will be easy to track. Probably the strongest signal of anyone in here. But what do I do when I get to them?'

'You won't get to them. Keep your distance. When you get sight of them, or a sense of them, report back to me like we discussed. I want to know where they are and in what direction they are headed.'

'Where are they going?' Davey asked, sensing that Zadie knew more than she was sharing. He wanted to do the right thing. If she saw his value and abilities, maybe he'd be the one she'd choose to be her right hand when the Given finally broke free of the underground and back into the world. She'd need someone with his skills if they were going to work alongside Jay and Stitch when the time came.

'We don't know where Cassie and Reuben are,' Zadie said. 'If they've been taken, they might be at the prison.'

'The so-called rehabilitation centre?'

'I don't know,' Zadie said. 'Look, don't get hung up on this. We don't know what's happened and we don't know where they are. We all have different senses, but none of us knows for sure. That's why Jay is out there looking. She should have been with you, and I need you to do as I have asked. Track, watch, and report back. Nothing more.'

'OK. That seems simple.'

'It's not. We can't afford to get this wrong. We need to know what side she's on.'

'What?' Davey interrupted.

Zadie didn't answer. She was edgy. This was not the time to push her.

'Do you understand your mission and do you have everything you need?' Zadie motioned towards the rucksack on his back.

'Yes and yes.' Davey nodded.

'Go.' Zadie nodded towards the doorway and Davey turned on his heels.

* * *

SAT on the edge of Stitch's bed, Zadie tried to get a sense of him. He was out there somewhere, with Jay, moving through the land. Together they were a formidable power, although Zadie couldn't help but think they'd not lived up to their potential. She'd had high hopes for Jay when she entered the Interland. She was supposed to be the one to define a clear path to emancipation of the Given – their victorious return to the world above, and the ultimate defeat of the Readers. How things had changed. The Given were extinct, but for the few remaining in hiding in their underground world. The Interland had become a virtual prison. She put a hand to the scar on the side of her face, and thought of Hinton.

When Zadie was first taken captive after the protest, she was held in the prison built for the Given. They interrogated her, but apart from Marcus, their most powerful Reader, their efforts to infiltrate her mind and take what they wanted were largely ineffective. Marcus had some power over her, but there was such energy when Marcus and Zadie were in the same place that their reality became somehow fractured and unstable. Time seemed to stutter and jerk. Marcus mostly left her alone after that, but then came Hinton – a far more terrifying individual than any Reader she'd come across.

Hinton was immune to her power, and she couldn't read him, couldn't influence him. He had a level of control over her that she couldn't fight or understand. He spoke softly to Zadie at first, as if he cared for her. He wanted her to come on side, to join him. The details of his mission were hazy back then, but the essence was clear: His desire was for her to stand with him so that they could together assume overall power. She didn't trust him, and she resisted.

Hinton was patient, but after Zadie had been in captivity for about a month, he grew weary. He turned and revealed his true self. He approached one morning without a word, entering Zadie's cell flanked by a group of five or six Readers. Then he dug into Zadie's consciousness. She tried to resist, but however hard she focused, she had little impact on the infiltration. The longer Hinton persisted, the weaker she became, until there was nothing but blackness.

She lost time. She woke days later in an unfamiliar wing of the rehabilitation unit. Her mind was scattered, her body weak. They wired her up to monitoring systems she was told could determine the level of any residual power. But she didn't need the machines to tell her what she knew deep down – that her power was gone. On her wrist was the merest of dark smudges where before there had been the number eight. On the side of her face was a scar from temple to chin. She didn't see Hinton again before she was released back into the community, no longer deemed a threat to the establishment, but she felt his presence. His face was in her head. The smell of his freshly pressed suit was in her nose. For weeks afterwards, it was as if, wherever she turned, he was with her – watching, reading, influencing.

The sense of powerlessness hurt Zadie far more than Hinton's act of reducing her. He had allowed her to live, but left her nothing to live for. She was weak and vulnerable to the growing presence of the Readers in society. It even crossed her mind back then that an alliance with Hinton might have been preferable to her gradual deterioration and eventual anonymous death.

Zadie was drawn to the hill forts, where the energy of the land was at its strongest. It was there she felt a spark of power, a seed that would grow with time. It took months to rebuild her strength, and her confidence. She'd regained much of her power by the time she got to the Interland, and with the concentrated energy of the source, she once more became the most powerful of the Given. That was until Jay and her connection to Stitch.

Zadie came across Hinton once more, a few months back. She had been out on a mission with two trainee Runners. She became separated from them as she followed her senses in search of one of the Given. Intelligence received at the Interland told that this person was in hiding in the suburbs in the south of the City. Zadie encouraged her trainees to follow their instincts – learn to read their senses and trust their feelings. They would learn to tune in to the energy of the Given.

Hinton drew her in. He somehow managed to confuse the signal of the power that she sensed, so that the energy of the Given that she thought she was tracking led her into an unfamiliar part of the City, away from the sanctuary of the hills. By the time she sensed the darkness, she was already in the heart of an area teeming with Readers. She could feel them.

She blindly followed her senses, walking past a row of disused houses. A pub on the corner was empty despite the enticing, warm glow emanating from its windows – the smell of hops drifted across her path. Continuing on her trail, she found herself in a dead-end alleyway around the back of the houses. The sense she had of the Given dissolved into the darkness to be replaced by the distinctive energy of the Readers. Zadie turned, and Hinton emerged from the shadows. The sight of him froze Zadie to the spot. Her heart raced as her eyes searched for an escape route. Readers lurked out of sight. Hinton was smartly dressed, as was his way, his immaculate presentation allowing him to hide his evil in plain sight. Without words, he guided her to the pub on the corner.

The proprietor placed two glasses of iced water on the table in front of Zadie and Hinton. Zadie looked at the man and immediately saw that he was a Reader, acting under the guidance of Hinton. He gave a smirk as he turned back to the bar, scuffing his feet as he went. She stared at the water for a moment, her throat parched. Condensation dripped down the side of the glass and the water seemed to fizz with an enticing glow.

'It's perfectly safe,' Hinton said, picking up his own glass, then placing it back down and taking Zadie's glass instead. He took a gulp of the water. Zadie immediately thought of the potential for a double bluff, but her thirst got the better of her and she took the remaining glass and drank. 'There,' Hinton said. 'Better?'

'What do you want?' Zadie asked, looking around and taking note of the location of the exits: two in the main bar, probably one in the saloon bar and then, if she was desperate, a potential for a window exit through the back.

'I thought we should talk. Like the two opposing Generals, meeting in no-man's-land to negotiate a truce.'

'A truce? Is that what this is?' Zadie instinctively tried to read him, despite knowing the futility of the effort. She searched her own mind for why he might be prepared for a truce. It was clear that outside the Interland, the control and dominance of the Readers was absolute. There were few remaining Given to offer any resistance, and the Readers had so infiltrated the heart of the State that the cause of the Readers and of Government were now synonymous.

'It could be. I see no reason to prolong the conflict.'

'That sounds more like a negotiation for our surrender,' Zadie said. She looked around the room once more, seeing that a number of Readers had entered, sitting at tables like any normal customer. Hinton undoubtedly had the upper hand. If Zadie was to get out of this situation, it would be if Hinton allowed it.

'Look.' Hinton leaned forward, his elbows on the table and hands together as if in prayer. 'In essence, we want the same thing. I believe there can be a world in which the Given stand alongside the Readers – a world in which you stand *with* me, not against me.'

'You've already shown how you treat the Given. Look at this place,' she nodded towards the window. 'It's been run into the ground. The Given are in hiding, or dead.'

'I'm not saying it couldn't have gone better. God knows I didn't wish for it to be like this. But we need to look ahead. We cannot even think about rebuilding society while this conflict remains – this impasse.'

'What do you propose?' Zadie said, finishing her water and leaning back to cross her arms over her chest.

'Like I said. A joint leadership. You and me, the faces of the Readers and of the Given. United.' Zadie shook her head in disbelief but her mind was already clasping on to the threads of the proposal as a viable route to the re-emergence of the Given – a route to consolidate her own power and control.

Zadie sighed, feeling a pinch in her chest as if her lungs were constricted. The weight of the energy of the Readers was becoming too much. 'Equal status? Readers and Given?'

'Of course,' said Hinton.

'What about the State?' asked Zadie. The rules of the State still said that the Given were illegal. Not just the *use* of their powers, but their very being.

'We *are* the State,' he said, a smile creeping over his lips.

Zadie saw little option at this point, and the possibility of a leadership position in driving the change required to establish the Given as equal partners was tantalising. But she was in no doubt that this man was not someone who could be blindly trusted. She would need some guarantees. 'How do I know you'll stand by your word?'

He smiled. 'I could have killed you back in that alleyway. In fact, I could have killed you before, when you were my guest in rehabilitation.'

'Guest?' Zadie scoffed. 'You reduced me. You took my power, my life force.'

'Dampened it. I didn't *take* it. Although I could have. It's returned to its full strength now?' Hinton seemed to smirk, as if he'd known that she would regain her power.

'You planned...' Zadie stumbled over her words. He had let her live. He'd reduced her to nothing, but he'd expected her to regain her strength. Why?

'I thought you'd come back, yes. I think we can be better together. With your influence over the Given, and my control of the State.'

'How? What's your plan?'

Hinton sat back, gathering his thoughts and his energy. 'With Jay and Stitch present at the Interland, we cannot integrate. Their connected power repels. It's divisive. We need to get Jay away from there. Only then can we open up the Interland to Reader and Given alike, and free the Given back to the world above. *Then* we can start.'

'The Given won't leave the Interland.'

'I thought you were their leader?' Hinton said. Zadie

shuffled in her seat and looked away from him. 'There will be some who will resist,' he continued. 'You will have to be strong and show leadership. Are you strong enough? Are you the one?'

'You know I am,' Zadie said.

He smiled. 'You are a born leader. But great leaders are made in the moment of choice under great stress.'

Zadie's initial anger at being manipulated soon dissipated as she saw a possible route to freedom in Hinton's plans. 'I'll consider it,' she said, standing to leave. Three of the Readers immediately stood, but Hinton signalled for them to stand down. Zadie made for the door without looking back.

PART II

10

I n the shadow beneath the bridge abutment, Jay pulled herself from the water. Stitch followed. Jay stood dripping onto the bank, staring off into the distance.

'What's up?' said Stitch, peeling off his wet shirt and replacing it with a dry one from his bag.

'Memories,' said Jay. The last time she'd been here, she'd narrowly escaped an attack from the Reader, Marcus. She pulled off her wet clothes with no self-consciousness. Stitch turned his back. He packed his own wet clothes away and scrambled up the bank to the village green. Jay followed, stepping onto the green and taking a deep breath, trying to settle her racing heartbeat. A conflict raged inside of her. The air smelled fresh outside of the underground, and the sun on her face warmed her cheeks, but an acute sense of anxiety rose in her chest. She felt vulnerable away from the source. She was detectable. And she was weaker. She held her breath for a moment to slow things down, to gain some control.

'Breathe,' said Stitch, placing a hand on her back.

'Sorry,' said Jay as she released the breath. 'Let's move.'

'Where to?' said Stitch.

'We need to get to Sidwell, to pick up the car.' Jay pulled a set of keys from her pocket, jangling them in front of Stitch.

'We're going in the Beast?'

'It's the only way to travel. But it's a good few hours' walk from here, so we need something to help us on our way.'

Stitch stepped into the road and held out his thumb as a car sped by without stopping. 'It's north, right?' Jay nodded.

They risked being picked up by a Reader, or someone unsympathetic to the cause of the Given. Jay had to make a choice. She decided that she'd feel the danger if it was significant, so set off along the road, her back to the oncoming traffic and her thumb out.

The anxiety they both felt about being exposed was diluted by the sense of freedom and beauty in the wide open space around them – the wind in the trees, and the fresh scent of the woodland. Jay had to squint in the light of day, her eyes used to darkness underground.

They walked for less than ten minutes before an old yellow Mini pulled in to the side of the road. Stitch jumped into the passenger seat, talking to the driver as Jay squeezed into the back.

'Sidwell?' the driver said. Jay gave some rough directions, and the man said that he'd be able to take them some of the way if not right into the village. He tucked a strand of his long, lank hair behind his ear and pushed a button on his car stereo to eject the cassette tape. He turned it over. 'You two alright with AC/DC?'

Stitch smiled, 'As long as we're heading north, we're alright with anything.'

Jay shuffled out of her rucksack and placed it on the back seat next to her, then lay with her head up against the door. She wound down the window, so the air flowed over her. Stitch and the man talked about music, the relative skills of various guitarists. Jay closed her eyes.

* * *

WHEN JAY WOKE, the car had stopped. Stitch and the driver were outside, sitting on the bonnet and sharing a cigarette. She gathered her things and pushed open the door. 'We here?' she asked.

Stitch turned and slid elegantly off the bonnet. 'Near as damnit,' he nodded in the direction of an overgrown pathway. Jay recognised it from when Cassie squeezed the car up the narrow track before it narrowed so much that it wasn't possible to get any further. Somewhere up there would be the Beast, her dad's old Ford. What were the chances of her being able to get it started after a year parked in an overgrown lane? 'Let's move,' said Jay.

Stitch held out a hand to their driver. 'Thanks, man.' He handed Stitch the cigarette and gave a brief wave to Jay before jumping back into the little yellow car and taking off.

'What's all the "Hey, Man" business?' asked Jay.

'What's with the attitude?' Stitch said. 'He was a champ, bringing us all the way here while you slept like a baby.' Jay gave Stitch a punch on the arm and they slung their bags on their backs and started off up the pathway.

They walked for just a few minutes before Jay recognised the opening to the field. The undergrowth had flourished, and on first glance Jay thought the car had gone. Looking again, it was clear that the bushes had grown over and around the car, hiding it from all directions.

'Crap.' Jay spat the word and kicked the front tyre. 'Now what?'

Stitch dumped his bag and began to clear the twisted branches and leaves away from the car door. 'Here,' he said, opening the door for Jay. She took out the keys and slipped into the driver's seat. She held her breath as she turned the key in the ignition.

Nothing. Not even a minor whir and turn of the starter motor. She caught Stitch's eye through the windscreen as he lowered his gaze and his shoulders slumped. Jay climbed out and looked up ahead of the car where the field fell away into a valley.

'Help me clear this stuff away and we'll bump it,' said Jay.

With most of the bush cleared from in front of the car and the wheel arches, Jay shoved at the back to get it rocking. It rolled a few feet. Jay pushed from the driver's side with the door open and Stitch assumed a similar position on the passenger side. The car rolled towards the top of the slope and began to gather speed. Its soft tyres made a grinding sound in the dirt. Jay jumped in first, followed by Stitch. Halfway down the slope into the valley, as the car reached nearly twenty miles per hour freewheeling, Jay looked at Stitch and put it into gear. The engine jolted. They lurched forward in their seats. The engine turned. Cylinders fired. Stitch gave a victory cheer as Jay revved the engine; black smoke poured from the exhaust. She smiled at Stitch and slammed it back into second gear, taking off down the slope towards the gate at the bottom of the field, through which their journey would begin.

11

——————

At the foot of Highdown, Jay and Stitch stood by the car, contemplating the climb. Jay was convinced this was where Cassie and Reuben had hit trouble, though the nature of the trouble evaded her. A dark feeling filtered through her.

'We need to climb,' Stitch said, intuitively understanding. Jay nodded, and they moved off together. 'Inside the ring of trees. That's where I can connect.'

At the halfway point, with Highdown directly in front of them, Jay climbed to a ledge to get a view to the other hill forts to the north and east at Cissbury and Chanctonbury. With sight of all three, the energy of the land was palpable. It flowed through her.

'It's strong here,' said Stitch.

Jay too felt the power coursing as strong as it did underground.

'Shall we try it?' said Stitch. 'Like back at the Interland. See if we can channel?' Usually their channelling was through the roots, the ground, the land, but the last time they had tried, Jay felt a human connection at the other end of their energy.

'Connect to the Interland?' said Jay.

'To whatever there is, let's see what happens.'

They both took a seat at the base of a large beech. Stitch took a deep breath. Jay looked up towards the summit of Highdown before taking Stitch's left hand in hers, holding him by his lower arm so that their wrists touched. Their sleeves were pulled back so that Jay's "8C" and Stitch's "C" physically connected. She closed her eyes and opened to the rush of energy.

A jolt of power and they opened their eyes, broke the connection. Both reeling.

'Again,' said Jay. Stitch took her arm and again they closed their eyes. This time Jay was ready for the flow. She channelled it and held tight to Stitch. She felt the power flowing and multiplying through Stitch's connection, as they had felt back at the Interland. Just as Jay felt her head might explode with the pressure and the heat that came from the energy, the power stabilised and took them down into the earth.

Jay moved through the roots of the great beech tree, into the ground through the fractured chalk. She moved through the subsurface aquifer, the groundwater that flowed to the edge of the dipping slope into the valley where it emerged as a river. Together, they entered the roots of the trees on the far slopes, climbing through the trunks and up into the branches, the leaves. Then down into the inner circle at the summit of Highdown, where there was a boy.

Stitch released his grip and fell back, away from Jay. Jay opened her eyes and gasped for breath, her chest burning with heat. She coughed, gagging. Stitch went to her, an arm around her shoulders. 'Breathe, slowly, breathe, Jay.'

Jay composed herself and looked up at Stitch, her eyes stinging. 'What the...?'

'I know,' said Stitch. 'Just slow down, breathe.' He went to his rucksack and pulled out a bottle of water, handed it to Jay and then picked out a packet of biscuits. 'Did you see him?'

'Was that real?'

'Felt like it,' said Stitch. 'A Reader?'

Jay shook her head. 'The colours. They weren't *Reader* colours. But he knows things. Could be one of the Given?'

'We need to get up there,' said Stitch, taking the water from Jay.

'Careful. He has power.'

'But not the darkness?'

'Maybe not,' said Jay. She smiled at Stitch, surprised at what they'd just achieved with their combined connection. 'That was pretty awesome.'

Stitch laughed, 'Did we just channel our consciousness through the environment?'

'There's something in the Sasha Colden history that hints at this kind of power,' said Jay.

'The biography?'

'Yes, but not in the words, in the subtext, like I was telling you. There are messages in there I can't explain. Can't describe how they come through. My grandmother, Sasha Colden, she did this, with her connection, whoever that was, she communicated through the earth.'

'You never said,' Stitch said, readying to head off, his rucksack tight over his shoulders.

'Not sure I knew until just now,' said Jay.

* * *

DARKNESS APPROACHED as Jay and Stitch climbed the final few metres towards the inner circle of trees atop Highdown. As the summit came into view, Jay immediately sensed the presence of Cassie and Reuben, and the taste of something deathly. Someone had died on the hilltop.

She glanced at Stitch. He felt it, too. They reached the edge of the inner circle and Stitch fell to his knees. 'Oh my god. They're dead.'

'Not Cassie,' said Jay. 'But Reuben...' Jay walked to the east edge of the trees. Stitch pulled himself up from the ground and scuffed through the grass after her. 'He died here.' She nodded at the ground where she felt that Reuben's life had slipped away into the earth. Her heart sank in her chest. She and Reuben were not close, but he was a good guy, a role model for the younger people in the Interland, and he was Cassie's first love.

'How do you know?' a voice from behind the trees startled Jay, and she instinctively stepped away, opening, scanning, ready to defend, or attack.

'Who are you?' called Stitch.

'My name is Otis,' the voice replied.

'The vision was real,' said Stitch. 'That's him.'

Jay couldn't deny that the boy they'd seen through the earth from across the valley was standing before them. His frizzy afro-hair, his scruffy clothes and over-sized jumper, his stubble, almost a full beard making him look older than the underlying truth that was a boy of no more than seventeen or eighteen years.

'I'm Stitch.'

Jay scowled at Stitch, not sure that they should engage with this boy. They knew nothing about him. And here he was in the location where Reuben had been killed and their best friend had been taken, and may also be dead by now. Jay couldn't read him. His shield was strong, but she dug, chipped away until she opened a crack, or he allowed her a look. He projected no hostility.

She saw he had buried Reuben's body.

Otis motioned for Jay and Stitch to follow him back into the inner circle of trees, entering the copse through a particular opening, an opening that Jay saw as reflecting the entrance to the ancient iron age settlement beneath their feet. He took a seat on a log beside a smouldering fire in the centre of the copse, waiting for Jay and Stitch to join him.

'I saw it happen,' Otis said as Jay took a seat on the opposite side of the fire, choosing to keep her distance.

'Saw what?' asked Stitch.

'Did you know them?' Otis asked. 'The boy, and the girl. They were up here the other night when the Readers came.'

'How?' Jay said. 'How did you manage to be here to see them when there were Readers up here? Unless you're working with them, of course?'

Otis smiled, a thin smile.

'What happened?' said Stitch. 'Tell us what happened to our friends.'

Otis looked at Jay as if for permission. Jay nodded, and he began: 'This is my place,' he said. 'I've been up here for months, a camp over the ledge there,' he nodded to the north. 'The only place I can get any peace, somewhere they leave me alone and I can see them coming a mile off. I get the occasional Reader up here, I can deal with that.' He looked at Stitch, then to Jay. 'I can shield, you see. Better than most, as you've probably figured yourself. I can tell you've got power. More than I've felt from any Reader.' Otis held Jay's eye, but she said nothing. 'I get power up here. I can keep my shield strong. I'm always topped up, so to speak.' Jay knew the benefits of Highdown for the powers. Her own energy levels were high.

'There was a Reader here?' said Stitch.

Otis nodded, 'Oh yes. There were loads of them that night. It was like a Reader gathering. Maybe twenty?'

'Why?' said Jay. 'What were they doing up here?'

'I think they were here for your friends. They arrived a couple of hours before and waited. I was up there.' He nodded proudly up into one of the largest trees that formed the inner ring. 'Biggest test for my shield. Not one of them sniffed me out. Weird thing was, the one in charge had no power. He was all suited-up like a banker or a politician or something. Shirt and jacket and all that, but no power. He had the lot of them in his pocket, though. Barely said anything and they followed him around doing his bidding without a word. Like the pied piper.'

Jay stood and walked around the fire, trying to gather her thoughts. 'How do you know they were here for our friends?'

'Because they moved in as soon as your friends turned up and came into the circle.' Otis relayed to Jay and Stitch the subsequent events. How Reuben was shown no mercy, and Cassie debilitated by the concentrated attack from at least three of the Readers, probably more.

'Why didn't you help them?' asked Stitch, standing, pacing.

'There'd be more than one dead if I'd tried anything.'

'They knew,' said Jay. Stitch frowned at her. 'Somehow, they knew that Cassie and Reuben would be up here, and they took the opportunity to take down two of the strongest of the Given.'

'Strongest?' said Otis.

'Both level seven,' said Stitch, his eyes lingering on Otis to see if he understood. The expression on Otis's face told Jay that he knew all about the power levels.

Jay looked around the perimeter of the trees, half expecting that they were being watched as they sat in the middle of the copse, in plain view. Stitch stood and followed Jay's gaze around the trees.

'There's no one here,' said Otis.

'You don't know that,' said Jay. 'If they can ambush Cassie and Reuben, then they can ambush anyone.'

'I've been up here for long enough to be able to read even the smallest changes in the signals. That night, when your friend was killed, I'd sensed those Readers way before they got here. Sensed your friends, too.'

He paused, frowning.

'What's wrong?' said Stitch.

'You two kind of confused me a bit. You were coming from all directions at once. Thought you were coming at me from the ground, or through the sky at one stage. Thought I was losing it.'

'Where do you think they took Cassie?' Stitch said to Jay.

Jay opened her mouth to respond, but Otis got there first. 'To rehab,' he said. 'The central rehabilitation unit. That's where they take all the Given.'

'Where my dad was,' said Jay.

Otis looked up, his eyes wide. 'You're Jay?' he said, looking from Jay to Stitch and back again. 'Your dad was in the stage one of rehabilitation when he broke out. You're Jay. The level eight with the "C". Can I see it?' He looked towards her wrist.

Jay kept her wrist covered. 'How do you know who I am?'

'Everyone knows. He's Stitch. Well, there are rumours.

You two are a legend for those of us still up here. The level eight and the connected. You give hope.' Otis stared at Jay. 'Or at least *used* to.'

'Stop talking,' said Jay.

'People say you went to the Interland. Is it true? You've been there?'

Jay and Stitch exchanged a glance, and Stitch said, 'It's not...'

'Don't say any more,' Jay interrupted.

'So it is true. I knew it was. And is Zadie Lawrence there too? She disappeared. Not a whisper. All the Given stuck out here, left behind to be picked off by Readers. No room in the Ark I guess?'

'It's not like that,' said Stitch, ignoring Jay's glare. 'It's not a place to inhabit. It's a place to regroup and make a plan.'

'Plan for what?'

'How to fight back,' said Stitch. 'To stand up against the oppression, the Readers.'

'What's the plan?' said Otis, a cynicism entering his voice.

Stitch looked into the fire. 'The plan is survival for now.'

Jay said, 'You said something about all the Given stuck out here? How many?'

Otis shook his head. 'Who knows? We all stay deep undercover. Most prefer to be alone. Less likely someone's going to turn you in for whatever benefits are on offer from the Readers.'

'We need to stick together,' said Stitch.

'Easy for you to say, from the comfort of your sanctuary.'

'But there's a network, right?' said Jay. 'Links between you all on the outside. You can communicate?'

Otis looked up into the trees. 'Kind of. You need

someone with more power than me to communicate wide. Not that we'd want to connect any more. Too dangerous, and what's the point?'

Jay scratched her head in frustration, standing up and wandering towards the edge of the circle of trees. At the time Jay had entered the Interland, she knew almost nothing about the extent of the oppression of the Given. Even without their leader, Marcus, there was little to stop the Readers and the State squeezing out any of the Given who they couldn't *rehabilitate*.

'What level are you?' asked Stitch.

Otis pulled back his sleeve and showed the number five on his wrist. 'Five?' Stitch said, his mouth remaining open. 'I thought there weren't any level fives?'

'Clearly,' said Otis.

'Alfred said...' Stitch looked to Jay for support.

'Alf's not always right,' said Jay. To Otis: 'So you can shield, we've seen that. What else does a level five have that we don't?'

Otis shrugged. 'Nothing I've figured out.'

'Or nothing you're prepared to share?' said Jay. Her trust in Otis was thin and getting thinner the more time she spent with him. He was hiding something.

'I could come with you?' said Otis. 'Help you find your friend, then go back to the Interland with you?'

Jay shook her head. 'No. We don't know what we're up against yet. And we don't know anything about *you*.' She stood and motioned for Stitch to stand with her.

Otis said: 'There's something coming if my senses are serving me.'

'Like what?' said Stitch.

Otis remained silent. He stroked his beard.

'Look after yourself,' said Stitch, stealing a glance at Jay as if suggesting they take Otis with them. Jay walked away with no acknowledgement of his look.

Otis stood and looked at Stitch, then turned to head back into the trees. 'Good luck.'

12

J ay gazed into the fire but it held no answers. She looked at Stitch, a deep frown etched his forehead, but she couldn't read what was troubling him.

'What's wrong? I feel you're worried about more than the gang of Readers Otis mentioned,' said Jay.

Stitch stirred from his thoughts. 'It's my dad. Something's wrong.' He stood and looked towards the coast. 'I need to see him.' Stitch had been close with his dad at one time, before they drifted. Their connection remained strong, and Stitch often felt his dad's emotions from a distance.

'We can't,' Jay said. 'You know this. If the Readers can pre-empt Cassie and Reuben like they did, we're next.'

Stitch avoided Jay's eyes. He'd already decided. He punished himself for abandoning his dad back when they left the first time. He would not ignore this call for help. 'I'll come with you,' Jay said. 'I'll go see Mum. One hour. No more.'

'What about him?' Stitch nodded towards where Otis had run off into the trees.

'He's hiding something. I don't trust him. The Readers might already be on their way here for us.'

'I don't think so,' said Stitch.

* * *

As Jay manoeuvred the Beast around the corner onto Stitch's street, she turned off the lights and drifted to a stop a few houses short of Stitch's house. All was quiet. A ginger cat crossed the road in front of the car and leapt onto a shallow wall.

'Henry,' said Stitch, his tone soft.

'Henry the cat?'

'Old bugger. Soppy as anything.'

The neighbour's house was dark, but Stitch's dad's place had a light on upstairs. Jay said, 'Looks like he's up?'

'That's the bathroom light. He always leaves it on at night. He's scared of the dark.' Stitch looked up and down the street. 'Look at this place,' he said. 'Half the houses are boarded.' He pointed across the road. 'That's Phil and Sarah's place. It's empty.'

'Things have got bad,' said Jay.

'I thought it was just the cities.'

'So what are you gonna do?' asked Jay. 'It's midnight. Are you going to wake him up for a chat?'

Stitch opened the passenger door. 'I'll see.'

'Let me know when you're done.' Jay tapped the side of her head. 'If I don't hear anything, I'll be back here at 1am sharp. Be ready.'

Stitch closed the door and gave a salute before silently sloping away towards the house. Jay watched him retrieve a key from under a plant pot and open the door.

Outside her mum's house, Jay sat in the car looking at

the kitchen window. The houses here were in a similar state to Stitch's. Almost half looked empty, neglected, some of them with chipboard covering the windows. The economy had deteriorated far more than they'd realised from the shelter of the Interland.

The kitchen light was off, but through the kitchen window, Jay saw blue light, could make out flashes of images from the TV in the lounge.

With a sigh, Jay stepped out of the car and gently clicked the door closed. She bypassed the front of the house, choosing instead to take the pathway around to the back. She shinned up the tree and onto the roof outside of her old bedroom window. The Velux was closed; she had to prise it open with her fingers. It swung on its centre hinge. She climbed in, breathing in the familiar scent of her room. Her bedroom was tidy, not like the Readers had left it after turning it inside out to find her dad's notebook. Now, there was nothing out of place. Her bed had been made, the duvet carefully turned back. She sat, running her hand over her soft pillowcase, its freshly washed scent taking Jay back to how it was before. She recalled the closeness with her dad and Sammy, her mum's distaste at everything she did, everything that Sammy did. The old bitter feelings came back.

Floorboards squeaked downstairs. Her mum must be heading to bed. It was a quarter past midnight, forty-five minutes to go until she needed to be back at Stitch's house. If she kept quiet for a moment, gathered a few of her things – a book, a notepad – then she could sneak back out to the roof until it was time. The thought of seeing her Mum made her feel uneasy, a task to be avoided.

Instead, Jay crept out onto the landing. She leaned over the railing to glimpse her mum as she made her way from the bathroom to her bedroom. She had curlers in her hair.

She looked older. She'd lost weight in the year since she'd last seen her, and her hair had greyed. The bitterness faded. Jay felt sorry for her mum. She was alone.

She stepped out from the shadows and Sonia let out a little scream, stepping back into the wall and bringing her hand to her mouth. As she recognised her daughter, her expression softened and her hand returned to her side. From a distance, Jay could see that her mum's eyes had welled with tears. 'Hi, Mum.'

'Jay,' she breathed Jay's name as if in awe.

'How are you?' said Jay.

'Ten years off me, you scaring me like that.' Her voice slurred a little, she'd been drinking.

Jay forced a half smile. 'Sorry,' she said.

'Come down, we can have tea?'

Jay hesitated. Only when her mum moved away towards the top of the first floor stairway did Jay move down the loft stairs, as if she needed to keep a steady distance between them.

Jay followed the noise of the kettle into the kitchen where her mum stood up against the work surface, wiping a tear from her eye with the back of her hand. She turned away from Jay, taking two mugs from the cupboard and scrabbling with an unopened box of tea bags. Jay was surprised at the emotion in her mum's face. Sonia Macfarlane, the mum she'd always known, was as hard as a rock, emotionless, spiteful. This woman seemed broken.

'I knew you'd leave,' Sonia said. 'Can't say I blame you.' Jay pulled herself up to sit on the worktop, legs dangling. Sonia continued, 'Where are you living?'

'I'm safe.' There were things she needed to keep secret for her mum's sake.

'Thought as much. You don't just vanish off the face of

the earth. The police were no use. They got all excited for a bit, even put officers outside the house. I reckon they thought I'd buried you all under the patio.' The kettle clicked and the sound of the boiling water subsided. Sonia remained still, staring at the mugs. Then she poured, her hand a little shaky as she held the kettle. Jay struggled for words. This was not the woman Jay remembered.

'The others? Your dad, Sammy? Are they OK?'

'They're fine. Look, Mum, we had to leave. It wasn't you. It's complicated. There were people looking for us.'

'Your dad,' Sonia snapped. 'People were looking for *him*, not you and Sammy. Your dad's the criminal, breaking out of that place. He's the one they wanted. Why'd he have to take you and Sammy?' She turned away from Jay, stifling tears. She opened a drawer and pulled out a teaspoon. Jay reached for the fridge and retrieved the milk, handing it over as her mum avoided eye contact.

'The Readers,' said Jay. 'It was the Readers. That's why we had to go.' Jay read her mum for the first time since entering the house. She'd been trying to avoid it, to keep things on an even level. Her mum did not know that Jay had power, that she was one of the Given, like her dad. She saw her mum's thoughts race around Jay's words: the *Readers*. Her mum knew all about the Readers. Jay wanted to ask about Marcus, how Sonia had got mixed up with him.

'I know about Marcus,' said Jay.

Sonia looked Jay in the eye and revealed everything in her thoughts. The man with the scar, the Reader who tried to wipe Jay off the face of the planet. Marcus. Her mum still had feelings for him. He was Sammy's biological father, there was no doubt about that, although her dad and Sammy never talked about it. But the man in her mum's thoughts was a quiet, unassuming gentleman - not the ruthless Reader who Jay had battled with.

Sonia lowered her gaze. 'He was kind back then,' she said. 'He worked for the State. Probably still does.'

'He was a Reader,' said Jay.

Sonia shook her head. 'Not back then. Well, at least they weren't called Readers back then, more like civil servants,' she smiled. 'He was a government official if you like. He had a good job, he was making a difference, and he was heading for the top of his profession...' Her words trailed off. 'Not like your dad,' she said under her breath.

He got to the top alright, Jay thought to herself.

'I kind of hoped Sammy might get some of his drive, you know. Not your dad's fantasy thinking,' she said, a bitterness returning to her voice.

'And not like me, I guess?'

'No,' her mum said. 'I didn't mean that. You don't know what it was like with your dad.' She stirred the tea, adding sugar to her own mug. 'You still have sugar?' she asked.

'No.'

Her mum squeezed the tea bags on the side of the mugs and dropped them into the bin under the counter. Handing Jay her tea, she said, 'So, has he? Sammy. Has he any of the power like Marcus?'

Jay didn't want to gratify her mum with the knowledge that Marcus's precious genes might have got through to Sammy. 'The powers aren't passed on through genes.' Jay sipped her tea. 'Genes might be a factor, but not the major factor. In truth, it's possible that a lot of it is environmental. People don't know for sure. And anyway, he's not 18 yet, so we wouldn't know.'

'He'd know by now.' Sonia deflated a little.

Jay shook her head, instinctively looking up and out of

the window for any signs of movement, aggressors, Readers. She could see the car up against the kerb outside. No sign of any life. 'So how have you been?' Jay asked. 'The streets are empty. Half the houses are boarded.'

'It's this recession. That's what you get from all the protests, the unrest. It does nothing for the economy. When will people realise we need to work together to get through these times? We need to support the State, all push in the same direction.'

'Whatever that direction is?'

'You sound like your dad,' Sonia said, turning to head out of the room. 'Shall we sit down?'

Jay followed and took a seat on the sofa. 'I'm sorry, Mum. I should have been in touch.'

Sonia put her tea down and stepped towards Jay, her arms outstretched. Jay stood for a moment and accepted her mum's embrace. She could smell chardonnay and menthol cigarettes. She hugged her mum for the first time in as long as she could remember. It felt like a dam might burst inside her body, emotions coming crashing through. She felt her mum tremble in her arms, stifling a sob. They stepped apart and sat at opposite ends of the sofa. Jay looked out the back window into the darkness and relaxed a little, sinking back into her seat, cradling her tea.

'They told me to contact them if you came back, if I heard from any of you,' said Sonia.

'Who told you?'

'The authorities. After I had the police out looking for you three, I got a visit from the suits. They were here for the best part of an hour. I felt washed out by the time they left, had to spend a day in bed.'

Jay imagined the work the Readers would have done on her mum, scraping her thoughts, asking questions and pulling information from her head without her knowing. 'What did you say to them?'

'I told them I'd let them know if I heard from you.'

'And will you?' Jay said.

Her mum shook her head. 'There's no way I'd have shopped you then, and I won't now. I've not done everything the way I'd have liked, I'll give you that, but I wouldn't want those lot getting hold of you and Sammy. They said they'd be in touch, that they'd keep a look out for you all.'

'They looked out for us alright,' Jay said.

'What?' Sonia asked.

Jay shook her head and smiled at her mum, seeing the humour in the way she looked with curlers in her hair. She laughed. 'Loving the curlers, Mum.'

Sonia raised her hand to touch her hair like she'd forgotten she had them in. 'Oh my life, sorry, I must look a state.' She laughed.

Jay smiled to herself. Her mum was different. The *house* felt different, as if released from the tension of her childhood. She sipped her tea and talked to her mum about Sammy, about how he'd met a girl who might be good for him. She told her about Cassie and Stitch, how the three of them had become closer than ever. As they talked, Jay relaxed further, and thoughts of the Readers dissolved into the darkness outside. She felt safe again, in her own home.

13

J ay slipped into the alleyway that led to Stitch's house. She'd left her mum's house in a hurry after waking from an unplanned snooze. Sonia had looked hurt at Jay's rapid departure, but she had no choice.

She broke into a run. She could sense power and her blood pumped hard. She crouched to get a look at the house and saw Readers, six or seven of them. They were paired, organised, each group with a fixed position, military-style. Jay stepped back into the cover of darkness to gather her thoughts. Everywhere ran a strong, dark presence of Readers.

Jay and Stitch had often used the hatch as a route into the basement, an old chute for coal that doubled as a perfect access and escape, out of sight of nosy parents. It was never locked when they were kids. It was locked now.

She caught sight of a gardening trowel and rammed it between the patio and the hatch, levering it up. The lock gave way with a loud crack and Jay ducked, sure someone must have heard the noise. All quiet, she swung the hatch open and slid down the chute and onto the concrete floor as the hatch clunked closed behind her.

It was so dark Jay couldn't see her hand in front of her face. She found the stairs, the sliver of light creeping through the door at the top enough for her to see to climb. She took it slowly. In the silence of the basement, each creak of the wooden steps was a thousand times louder in her head. She paused at the top, listening. Voices drifted through from upstairs, but she couldn't make out the words. There was no one in the kitchen, at least no one with power.

The kitchen was empty. Voices came from the front of the house, the front door where Readers moved in and out, passing information, preparing to take Stitch away. 'What about the girl?' a voice said.

'Orders are to finish the boy and head back to base.'

'Leave the girl?'

'A unit is on its way to her mother's house.'

Jay strained to hear the response. A loud crack, the sound of a gun, reverberated through the house, followed by shouting from upstairs. Readers bolted up the stairs. Jay slipped from the safety of the basement, through the kitchen and to the foot of the stairs. She followed a few feet behind, then stepped into a doorway, out of sight. She heard Stitch's dad shouting in Arabic and Stitch, trying to calm him down.

A violent shove from behind and Jay almost lost her footing, spilling onto the landing and slamming into the banisters. A Reader's hand reached for her; she ducked away and opened her mind in readiness to attack. Before she could infiltrate, a heavy thump on the back of her head sent her to the floor. Hands pulled her to stand and shoved her into one of the bedrooms.

'Jay?' Stitch's voice.

She touched the side of her face where she'd knocked it on the floor. A little blood. Nothing serious. A Reader pushed Jay and Stitch back against the window, next to Stitch's dad, Samir.

'Well, what a lucky day,' said one of the Readers.

Jay tried to see the number on his wrist. She sensed he was a six. A group of sixes would be too strong for her and Stitch unless they could get some time to channel their power. But these Readers knew that. They were poised to attack, to knock them down at any sign of power.

They were all crammed into Stitch's bedroom, a room in which Jay had spent a big part of her childhood. It still smelled of his deodorant. Over her shoulder, Jay sensed a white glow coming from the back garden and she turned.

'Eyes on me,' the Reader shouted at Jay, but his shouts trailed off as he caught sight of the glow.

A man crossed the grass, a magical white glow all around him. Jay looked at Stitch, and then to Samir. Both were transfixed. The Reader stepped towards the window, pushing Jay and Stitch aside.

'What is it?' Stitch whispered to Jay. Jay shrugged. Three more Readers entered the room, one of them shouting to the leader to move out with Stitch and Jay. But he too trailed off at the sight of the white light now pouring over the back of the house and in through Stitch's bedroom window.

The Readers were transfixed by the vision. They stared for a moment and then edged backwards, away from the window. The light intensified and seemed to shimmer around the Readers in the room, forcing them back and out through the door. Jay watched as they left. She looked back to the garden, where Stitch and Samir continued to stare. The glow subsided, leaving Jay's eyes struggling to focus.

With the retreat of the glow, the figure of the man was gone.

'What was that...' Stitch said.

'*Madha? 'ana la 'afham*,' breathed Samir.

The Readers had retreated to the ground floor. Voices from downstairs grew louder in argument. Jay nudged into Stitch. 'We need to go. How do we get out?' Stitch looked towards the stairs. 'Not that way,' said Jay.

'There's a balcony on Dad's room, we can jump. Follow me.' Stitch bolted.

Samir followed with Jay close behind. She heard heavy footsteps rushing up the stairs. The three of them slipped into Samir's bedroom as the Readers piled back into Stitch's room, now empty. There were shouts, orders to find them. Stitch edged out onto the balcony.

''*ana kabir fi alsini ldhlk*,' Samir said, stepping out onto the ledge with his son, then he jumped, a clean landing turning into a forward roll. Stitch smiled at Jay, shrugged, then jumped, following his dad into the darkness. As Stitch scrambled to his feet on the grass below, the door of the bedroom slammed against the wall. Two Readers fell into the room and caught sight of Jay. Jay turned and threw herself off the balcony, landing heavily and sprawling onto the grass. She scrambled to her feet and ran towards the back fence where Samir was already up and over, Stitch close behind him. Jay sat astride the top of the fence just as the first Reader landed in the back garden and another three came into view, running around the side of the house from the front. She slid down the fence, catching and grazing her shin on the shiplap. She cried out. Stitch turned and Jay waved him on. 'End of the alleyway, go,' she shouted. She bit her lip and swallowed the pain, taking off after Stitch.

'Keys,' said Stitch, holding out his hands as Jay turned the corner. She pulled them from her back pocket and threw them. He fumbled at the passenger door as Samir doubled over, catching his breath. Jay ran around to the driver's door, looking back down the alleyway as she slammed into the car.

'Stitch,' she said, seeing three Readers powering down the alley towards them. 'We need to leave. Like... now.'

Stitch got the door open, jumped in and leaned over to open Jay's door and then into the back to unlock the door for Samir. The three escapees each locked their doors from the inside as Readers descended on the car, pulling at the handles. Jay fumbled with the keys. The Reader at the back of the car stopped pulling at the door and Jay saw out of the corner of her eye that he was trying to dig into Samir, influencing. Samir turned towards the Reader, his expression neutral.

'Jay...' Stitch said.

'I know,' said Jay, at last getting hold of the ignition key.

'Jay...' Stitch repeated, watching his dad as he stared at the Reader. Samir's hand moved towards the door lock as if he were about to open it.

'Jay!' Stitch screamed, launching himself towards the back door to stop his dad unlocking it.

'I know,' Jay shouted, the engine catching just as Samir had switched the door catch. Two of the Readers pulled at the handle, the car already moving. The door swung open and one of the Readers managed to get a hold on Samir's top, holding tight as the car gathered speed. Stitch grabbed at the Reader's hand, prising his fingers from Samir. Jay put her foot down, the front wheels of the old Ford turning in the gravel until they gained traction and the car lurched forward. The Reader's hand was yanked away, strands of

Samir's top remaining in his fingernails. The car swung around, and the door slammed shut, Samir slumping back into his seat and Stitch lying prone halfway between the front and back of the car.

14

The heavy door swung slowly inwards with a clunk, startling Cassie. Hinton peered inside before ushering one of his Readers to a position in the corner of the room.

'What's he for?' said Cassie, remaining seated.

'Wouldn't want you getting any ideas about roughing me up, would we? I hear you have some skills in that department?'

Cassie had already thought about it, but she was so weak she could barely stand. 'What do you want with me?'

'Nothing,' he smiled. 'You're our guest. Think of this as your weekend away, your countryside break from a life underground.' The Reader laughed, and Cassie lowered her gaze. She would avoid meaningful conversation, focussing simply on regaining strength. 'Seriously though, Cassie. You're here to help entice your friend Jay for a visit.' He gestured around the room. 'You think she'll like it here?'

'She won't come here.'

'How can she resist? You're giving off a distress signal as we speak. The wonderful thing about my little invention here, is its functionality in re-radiating the energy. Inside here, the metal *reflects*. Not only will she sense you, but that signal is amplified.' He laughed. 'Even Jay won't be able to resist, however scared she is. She'll smell you out like you're a skunk on overdrive. What do you think?'

'I think Jay and Stitch will take your head off.'

'Stitch? He won't be troubling us anymore.'

Cassie looked at Hinton, dismissing any attempt to read him. Stitch can't have been taken prisoner. She'd have felt it. If he'd been killed, she'd have sensed it for sure. Still, doubt crept into her mind. She was sitting in a steel box, after all. 'Why are you doing this?'

Hinton paced the room, a half smile on his face.

She could feel his desire to brag, to boast about his wonderful plans, but he hesitated.

'You've got nothing,' Cassie said. 'This is just your personal little crusade. You're weak. No power, no plan.'

'Hush,' he whispered. 'You're just bait. Jay's the one we need in here, and now that Stitch has gone, there's nothing to get in our way.'

'Then what?' said Cassie.

'Then it's a little journey to the Interland, to the source, to see if we can put an end to the powers. For good.'

'Your lot need the source as much as the Given...'

'Not true,' Hinton interrupted. He smiled, unable to contain himself. 'Readers draw power from somewhere else,' he said, almost a whisper. 'So, you see, once the source has been destroyed, there's nothing else to threaten the leadership, and the only thing between us and the source is already on her way here, thanks to you.'

15

J ay pulled the car into the car park at Highdown, while Stitch and Samir slept. No one had spoken since they left Stitch's house just an hour before. They were in a daze, exhausted and confused. Jay was naturally drawn back to Highdown, her thinking space, but she felt no pull to climb to the summit. She wound her seat back, closed her eyes and fell asleep almost immediately.

It was light when Jay woke. She rubbed the sleep from her eyes and peered through the windscreen. Stitch was sat on a bench at the edge of the car park smoking a cigarette. Samir snored in the back seat. Jay closed her car door gently so as not to wake him; the sweet sound of birdsong reminded her of Sammy. Toyah called him the *sparrow whisperer*.

Stitch nodded as she took a seat next to him on the bench.

'What happened back there? What was that thing? It was like a ghost or something?'

They remained silent for a minute, looking up into the

trees that peppered the slope in front of them. Jay shook her head slowly. 'More like a mirage, or a projection. Did you feel it?'

'Saved our arses.'

'I think that was the point,' said Jay. 'We have a guardian angel.'

'Who?'

Jay shrugged, 'Search me. Not from the Interland. Zadie doesn't have that kind of power.'

'No one has power like that,' said Stitch, flicking his cigarette end into the grass. 'It was weird. I can't get it straight in my head, but it was like the ground opened up and we were on the edge of something.'

'I felt that too. A wider connection. Whatever it is, it's helping us. It pushed those Readers away.'

'What about *him*?' Stitch said, nodding up at the slope. 'Otis. You think he came to our rescue?'

Jay shook her head, but Stitch pressed, 'He's a level five. If Alf's right, they have a different sort of power.'

'No way. That boy's a loner.'

Stitch looked sideways at Jay. 'I don't think we should disregard him. He could help.'

'I'm not sure we can trust him.' Jay shook her head again, and spoke firmly. 'Someone knew where we were going last night.'

Stitch remained quiet for a minute. 'Something is twisted in the energy of this place, but it's not him,' he said.

'What do you mean?'

'I don't know. Just a feeling. Twisted, dark, bitter. A feeling, a taste.' Stitch looked at Jay. 'You know what I mean,' he said, impatience in his voice.

Jay had felt it too, but it made no sense. What she felt was *Marcus*.

She took a breath and searched inside herself, her connection to the ground beneath her feet, the life that stretched through the earth. In her bones, she knew that Stitch was right.

Jay pushed Marcus from her mind and looked back at the car. 'What are we going to do with your dad?'

'We talked last night, before the chaos. It was good. He even spoke English for most of it. He reverts to Arabic when he's under pressure. I don't even think he realises he's doing it.'

'Instinctive,' said Jay.

'Against my better judgement,' Stitch said. 'We will need the old man if we're going to get through all the Readers at the prison.' He smiled, affection in his expression.

'Why?'

'Mum worked on that development. She knew the layout, and they talked about it. There might be a way in without attracting undue attention.'

'Good work, boys,' Jay said, feeling like it was about time they had a piece of good fortune. She stood to make her way back to the car. 'I'll grab a map. We can make a plan.'

16

Davey pulled off his crash helmet, careful to remain out of sight of Jay and Stitch. He leaned the motorbike onto its stand and stepped off. A man slept on the back seat and Davey recognised Stitch's dad. He'd been watching last night but hadn't intervened. He'd been under strict orders from Zadie to keep his distance. Observe and report.

He placed his crash helmet on the forest floor and pulled off his jacket. He took a seat on a log, a vantage point from which to watch over Jay and Stitch, still sat on the bench at the edge of the hill.

It was just three minutes until the pre-arranged time for his next communication with Zadie. He trusted Zadie with his life. She'd saved him. She took him in, trained him, supported him. If Zadie didn't trust Jay to do the job of finding Cassie, then she had good reason.

He looked again at his watch. It was time.

Clearing his mind, Davey connected to the source and to Zadie's consciousness. Without moving his lips, he described the events of the raid at Stitch's house, the white glow, their escape, and the scene in front of him now.

Tentatively, Davey asked Zadie what was going on. Should he join with Jay and Stitch, to support their mission to find Cassie and protect them from the sudden influx of Readers? The message he received was unequivocal. Keep to the plan. Observe, report back. The communication ended.

17

S ammy's head torch played beams of light and shadow against the rock walls of the tunnel. He was tempted to pull himself up through the roof opening into the Free Cave for some peace, see if he could get a little further along the uncharted passageways beyond the high ledge. But not without Toyah, he thought to himself.

The walk from his room in the residential section to the main cavern where food was served was only ten minutes. On the way, he passed the opening that led down to the source and felt its gentle pull. No one was allowed into the source rooms without the knowledge and supervision of a level eight which meant Zadie, now that Jay was out on a mission.

Zadie had become difficult to read. Sammy felt she was shielding. But why? He'd seen her in snatched, whispered conversations with some of her closest companions. If Jay were here, she'd quickly get to the heart of the situation by reading it, not allowing her imagination to do the talking the way Sammy did. The bottom line was Zadie Lawrence made Sammy nervous.

'Stuffing your face as usual?' Sammy said, taking a seat beside his friend Pinto.

'You want some?' Pinto said, pushing his plate towards Sammy.

Sammy shook his head. 'Where's Toyah?'

Pinto shrugged. He finished his food, using his bread to scrape up the last of the stew. 'You want to play?'

Sammy looked around. No sign of Toyah. Then back to Pinto. 'Chess?'

Pinto shook his head. 'Let's fly,' he said with a grin.

Despite neither of them having a marking yet, with Pinto, Sammy could connect and then project a common vision from a position away from their bodies. It was like generating a communal out-of-body experience. He'd tried it with Toyah, but it didn't seem to work with anyone but Pinto.

Sammy held out his hands. Pinto took them and they both closed their eyes. They had this process to connection well-honed. Sammy felt Pinto's energy matching his own as their bodies connected. A warmth filled Sammy's body. He allowed the energy to flow. Pinto had power, as much as his sister Toyah, if not more. Pinto's grip tightened on Sammy's hands and he could feel the warmth lifting him, elevate them both in mind.

Sammy saw himself from above, locked together with Pinto. He could see the tops of their heads, the smile on Pinto's face. Their connected mind's eye rose to the roof of the cavern and drifted further up towards the opening in the rocks. With Pinto's pushing and shoving, Sammy saw into the trees beyond the cavern. Like a bird, Sammy pushed down with a force that projected their vision further up into the rocks. He glimpsed the sun, felt a breeze on his face from the outside.

Back in the cavern, he opened his eyes and saw the grin still plastered on Pinto's face before he too opened his eyes. 'We could have gone higher,' said Pinto, releasing Sammy's hands and looking into the roof of the cave.

Sammy jumped to his feet. 'Hey, I'm hungry, follow me,' he said. He led Pinto through a narrow opening and into a side cavern that had been converted into a cooking area, with a series of open fire pits with makeshift chimneys in the roof. There were three people with their backs to Sammy and Pinto, preparing food for the evening meal. He turned to Pinto and put a finger to his lips as they crept through the room and continued to another opening. This next room was stocked with shelves full of food. There were tins, packets and all the things you'd expect to see in a supermarket in the outside world, collected by Runners. Then there were crates of vegetables and fruit, some home-grown in the allotments on the east side of the Interland, and some foraged from the outside world.

Sammy waved for Pinto to keep up as he made his way to the far end of the stores and knelt beside the sacks of rice. He shifted one of the sacks to the side to reveal a small opening, just big enough for someone to crawl through. Pinto peered inside, mouth open. 'Where does it go?'

'This passage connects up with the passages that lead to the Free Cave. I've used this passage to move between my room and the stores.'

Pinto shoved Sammy. 'No, you haven't. Why?'

'Midnight food run,' Sammy grinned, pulling a torch from his pocket and shining it into the opening. He was about to look away when he caught sight of something inside he'd not seen before. A stash of crates lined up against the wall of the tunnel.

'What is it?' asked Pinto.

Sammy moved further into the tunnel to see if he could read the writing on the side of the crates. 'Fertiliser,' he said.

Seeing crates of fertiliser wasn't necessarily strange given that they might use it for the allotments, but next to the crates were boxes with electronics, and a stash of batteries. Sammy knew well enough from the TV shows he used to watch in the outside world. This stuff was for making bombs.

'Hey.' A voice from behind them made Sammy jump and Pinto fall backwards. Sammy knocked his head on the ceiling of the tunnel as he tried to edge backwards in a rush.

It was Toyah. Sammy stood and smiled, a warm blush sweeping his face.

She put her hands on her hips and looked at her little brother. 'I've been looking all over for you, Pinto. You and me are on kitchen duty.'

'Look no further, I'm here. I was here before you,' Pinto said, storming out of the storeroom and into the kitchen where he plucked an apron from a hook on the wall. Sammy could smell chopped onions frying.

'What are you two up to?' said Toyah as Sammy shoved the rice sack back into place over the entrance to the tunnel.

'Nothing, just playing,' said Sammy. 'You want to do something?'

She motioned towards the kitchen. 'I'm on rota.'

'I'll help then,' said Sammy.

'Don't be stupid. Go and do something. It'll be your turn soon enough.'

Sammy shrugged. 'Later then?'

Toyah nodded and went to join Pinto as Sammy made for the exit.

* * *

On his way back to his room, Sammy saw Zadie emerge from the passageway that led down to the source. He ducked into an alcove in the wall so that she wouldn't see him. She stepped out from the passageway and headed in the direction of the main hall. As she disappeared around a corner, Sammy made his way down towards the source, an urge to head into the heart of the Interland.

Zadie had questioned Sammy, along with his dad, the morning Jay and Stitch had slipped out of the Interland. She had convinced Ben that sending Davey was the only way to keep Jay safe. His dad seemed to buy the story, but Sammy hadn't been convinced.

He followed the steps down to the lowest point of the Interland. He lit two of the candles and approached the three streams of water that bubbled as they came together and flowed away into the rocks below. There was something magical in the shimmering water: hints of colours and sparkles that gave a sense of the power within.

He placed his hand in the pool.

A shimmer of light filled the cave. He felt energy flow through him more than ever before. Whatever power he had was edging closer to the surface as he approached his 18th birthday. Sammy breathed in to the energy, accepted its connection. The light intensified, and he shielded his eyes. When his eyes finally adjusted to the light, he saw he was no longer inside the cave but soaring high above the trees on the outside of the Interland. He had the eyes of a bird.

His vision blurred. The trees below, the hills, and the wider landscape came at him in colours, like through a thermal lens. The trees shone yellow, the hills red, as he swept towards the coast. He recognised the River Arun, its meandering form shining orange, and swooped to follow its path towards the sea, moving faster than he could ever have imagined. Within seconds, he was above the estuary and turning to the east, along the coast. As he looked to the north, he saw the striking energy in the colours of the hills.

Then a dull ache filled his head as a shadow passed before his vision. The water and trees were tainted with an inky-black stain that lurked in the valleys between the hill forts on the downs, and spread in all directions, edging towards the hills, the coast, the Interland.

The piercing bright light returned. The hills, valleys and the landscape disappeared once more. Feeling came back to Sammy's legs just as they gave way and he slumped to the floor of the cave. The candles had been extinguished and the only sound was the trickle of the three streams of water meeting in the centre of the pillar. Sammy reached out his hands to feel for the wall, edging himself to stand. He felt his way to the foot of the stairwell, his mind still with the eye of the bird, soaring above the surface of the earth. He struggled to find meaning in the darkness of the valleys, the swirling black mist that threatened the Interland.

At the foot of the stairs, a chink of light penetrated from above, allowing him to balance himself. With a hand on the wall, and a pounding in his head, Sammy crept back up the steps.

* * *

IT WASN'T until the next day that Sammy finally tracked Toyah down to the reading room. The experience at the source had shaken him. He had lain awake most of the night, pushing thoughts and theories around his head. The darkness he saw hinted at a shift in the power. Without Jay, he had no way to decipher it. All he knew was that there was a growing sense that he needed to get away from the Interland. He needed to find Jay.

Sammy closed the book he'd been pretending to read and glanced at Toyah. 'Hey, do you think...'

Toyah interrupted him with a finger to her lips. She nodded towards the woman on the other side of the reading room with her head in a hardback. Sammy shrugged and Toyah again put her finger to her lips. He caught a slight smile on her face as she returned to her book. Her smooth, dark complexion was like her brother's, if a little darker. Her hair used to hang below her shoulders, but she'd cropped it a couple of weeks back, close to her head so that it was shorter than Sammy's own hair. Pinto had laughed when she'd had it cut, but Sammy had gasped. With nothing to hide her face, Sammy saw her genuine beauty. She was way too good for him. Two years older and a long way out of his league.

The woman on the other side of the room closed her book and returned it to the shelf before leaving. 'We have to go,' Sammy said.

Toyah looked at him quizzically. 'What? Go where?'

'Away from here,' Sammy said. 'I'm worried about Jay. I need your help.'

'You're kidding, right?' said Toyah, concern in her eyes. 'We're lucky to have found the safety of this place.'

Sammy sighed. He couldn't explain his feeling, he just knew. They were all in danger. 'Look,' he said. 'I think we should leave. We can get Pinto, and Dad...'

'Pinto and me are going nowhere.' She closed her book. 'Do you know what we went through to get here?' Sammy lowered his head, thinking that he *would* know if she'd trusted him enough to tell him. 'We spent half of Pinto's life finding this place,' she said. 'We're not leaving.'

Sammy could see it was no use arguing with her. He thought he might speak to his dad. Ben always knew what to do. But the distance that had opened up between them in the Interland made it difficult. Ben was not the father he'd grown up with. He needed to convince Toyah himself. He needed more proof.

The car cantered between the villages of the Downs, Jay making their way east to the prison. Samir had insisted on sitting in the front, relegating Stitch to the back seat. He asked question after question, trying to make sense of what Jay and Stitch were doing. Who were these Readers? Why were they pursuing his son?

'Why do they have your friend? What do they want with her?' Samir said.

'You've not spoken this much English since mum died,' Stitch said from the back of the car.

Samir said nothing, turning to the window. Jay looked at Stitch in the rear-view mirror. He shrugged.

Samir said, 'I'm sorry. It's been hard for you.'

'It's OK,' Stitch interrupted, placing a hand on his dad's shoulder.

Without shifting his gaze from the fields beyond his window, Samir reached to place his own hand over that of his son.

'We think they took her because she has power – simply because she is one of the Given,' said Jay.

'And then they killed her friend?' said Samir.

'Reuben,' Stitch said. 'Yes.'

A dark shadow moved at the side of the road. Before Jay could fully take it in, the car veered sharply, as if pulled into the verge by a magnetic force. She threw her weight into the steering wheel to keep it straight and the car on the road.

'What's wrong?' said Stitch.

'The car,' Jay gasped, 'I can't... hold... it.' Samir leaned across to help Jay hold the wheel. Jay slammed her foot on the brake pedal, but as soon as she did, the car pulled more dramatically to the left, overcoming both Jay and Samir. They ploughed through a fence, a hedge, and launched over a shallow ledge into a lake. Jay's last memory before everything turned white was of the tranquillity of the vast, still surface of the water and the silence inside the car. Samir slid back into his seat and Stitch slammed into his side door as the car twisted in the air.

There was no jolt as they hit the water. There was no sound.

* * *

JAY LAY face down on a hard, dusty-dry surface, stones digging into her torso and legs. She lifted her head and spat grime from her mouth. Stitch lay beside her. White light poured from the sky, bleaching everything so that Jay could see nothing more than a few feet around her, the rest of the landscape hidden inside the blinding light, a white glow like they had seen in Stitch's back garden. She shielded her eyes as the landscape took form.

They were on an island in the lake, no more than twenty feet across, surrounded by water. 'Dad?' called Stitch, his voice croaky and his legs unstable as he tried to get to his feet. He too shielded his eyes from the bright light. Stood together, the two friends gazed out across the lake, a surreal sense that they were not in the same world they'd left just a moment before.

There was no sign of Samir.

'Where's the car?' said Jay.

Stitch limped towards the shore. He scanned the perfectly smooth surface of the water. 'Where's the road?' All around them was nothing but water. No sign of an end to the lake, a road, hedge line, nothing. The landscape was the same in all directions.

'There,' Jay said, pointing to the distance, 'there's the shore.'

'That's another island,' said Stitch.

'And there,' said Jay, shielding her eyes in the light to see another small island, and another. 'There's a circle of them.' They stood on a small island in the middle of an apparently endless expanse of water, other small islands forming a circle around them, each island perhaps a hundred feet away from the next. On each island there stood a single tree, reaching from its centre into the sky. Nothing else but yellow dust and stones.

Stitch looked at Jay. 'Are we dead?'

Jay wobbled on her feet, and Stitch steadied her with a hand. 'Can you feel anything?' asked Jay. 'I mean power, energy?'

Stitch shook his head. 'Nothing.' He looked out across the endless lake. 'Dad!' he shouted.

'He's not here,' said Jay

'He must be! We have to find him.'

'I mean he's not *here*, in this place, or time, or whatever this is.'

Stitch looked distraught. 'What is *happening?*'

'This is *not* the place we just left.'

Stitch studied his shoes for a moment, then stroked his jumper as if trying to find out whether it was real, whether he was physically present. 'Maybe it's like up at Highdown? Like when we connected and travelled through the environment to that boy, Otis? This is like that?'

'I don't know,' Jay said, pacing the perimeter of the little island and looking up at the tree.

'There! Look!' said Stitch. Jay followed his gaze towards the island nearest to them. A white glow emanated from the foot of the tree and then fizzled and died. A figure stepped out from the shadow of the tree. It was a man, tall, skinny.

The man held a hand aloft in greeting. 'Jay? Stitch?'

Jay and Stitch looked at each other and then back to the man, coming into view as he approached the shore of his little island. Jay could see that he was a little older than them, perhaps late twenties or early thirties, with dark skin. 'Who are you?' said Jay. 'Where are we?'

'Sorry for the drama,' he said. 'I wasn't sure if this would be possible.' He scanned the lake and other islands. He had an accent Jay couldn't place – possibly South African. 'Can you see the source, on your island?' Jay and Stitch looked behind them, seeing only the tree. They looked back to the man, confused. 'At the foot of the tree, are there three streams of water coming from the centre of the trunk and down into the ground?'

Jay stepped closer to the tree and crouched. She dug with her hands until she felt dampness in the soil. She dug further until she exposed three streams of water, combining amongst the tangle of tree roots and soaking away as a single flow into the ground. 'Stitch, look,' she said.

Stitch joined her. 'Like at the Interland,' he said.

Jay stood and turned towards the man. 'What...? Where are we?'

'Is the source there?' the man asked.

'Yes, but...'

'Good,' he said. 'We can be thankful for that at least.' He pointed then, towards the islands on the other side of the circle, the ones furthest away. 'See there? Without the source, the island dies, like those three.'

Jay looked closer. Three of the islands in the distance were blackened as if scorched by fire. Their trees without leaves, trunks charred. 'What happened?'

The man waded towards Jay and Stitch until the water level reached his knees, and he stopped. 'Do you know where we are, Jay?' he called across the water.

Jay shook her head but then found herself saying, 'Yes.' She searched her mind for a name but again felt lost.

'It's not easy to explain in words. In fact, I think you might know better than me where we are. Personally, I think of it as a kind of inner space, where the energy of the environment combines with that of the people, but that's just the way my brain interprets it.'

'Why are we here?'

'Because I brought you here,' the man smiled.

'What for?' asked Stitch.

The man pulled back the sleeve of his left arm, showing Jay and Stitch the marking "8C". Jay stepped back. 'Same as me...'

'You thought you were the only one?' he said. Jay nodded, lost for words. 'Almost right. There are not many. Well, there are eight, exactly, and eight connecting partners like Stitch here.'

Stitch and Jay exchanged confused glances, the information slowly seeping into Jay's understanding, connecting the pieces of the jigsaw that had been there all along, just without coherence. Eight islands, eight sources, and eight people at level 8C. The man nodded at Jay as if reading her understanding. 'This is the first time I've been able to do this, to connect with another 8C in this physical way. You are the first one that's been strong enough, receptive enough.' He smiled, and Jay sensed his joy and excitement.

'I still don't understand why we are here?' Jay said, desperate to untangle her confusion.

He nodded towards the tree behind them. 'To stop your island from going the same way as those over there, so to speak. Which is what will happen if we don't stop what's coming.'

The blackened islands were charred and dead, shadowed in darkness.

The man sat down in the water so it came level with his chest and the tops of his knees. Stitch shot Jay a look that questioned the man's sanity. 'This place,' the man said, 'if it can be called a *place*, is a representation. I'm not sure if it's a construct of my head, my energy and power, or yours, or a combination. It doesn't matter, it comes from deep within, not from our conscious selves. The important thing is what it shows us.' Jay and Stitch remained silent, Jay looking around the lake at the other seven islands in turn, Stitch unable to drag his gaze from the man. 'See there?' The man pointed towards the water. A swirling stream of black water flowed between the two islands. The man stood, water dripping from his trousers. He stepped backwards until his feet returned to dry land. He continued to point at the sinister-looking black swirls, like black paint, or an oil slick drifting and swirling with the currents in the water.

'What is it?' asked Stitch.

'Three of the islands are black already. Five remain, but

the darkness is expanding. It's like a hunger.' The man kept his eyes trained on the swirling black streams in the water that flowed between their islands. 'It's not just in your country that the Given exist, you know that?' Stitch and Jay looked at each other and nodded. They knew of the power beyond their own country's shores, despite the State restricting information. And, through the source, they'd sensed a communication that went further. 'And, where you have the Given, you have Readers, if you have a manipulator.'

'A what?' said Stitch.

'Someone who controls them. A manipulator. Someone who transcends the power of the Given and of the Readers. Your manipulator has the power to reduce the Given, and control the Readers,' the man said. Jay thought about Marcus. His scar, originally generated by a reduction and a transformation that created a level eight Reader. Someone had transformed Marcus – the manipulator.

Zadie too had a scar to show that she had been reduced. But she was not transformed. She remained strong, rebuilt her power as one of the Given.

Jay looked at Stitch and saw the same question in his eyes. Had Marcus survived the attack at the Interland gateway?

'So a manipulator has Cassie?' asked Stitch.

'I think that's likely. But you need to see the bigger picture. Look around you. This darkness will soon consume all our islands, and all of our lands will be lost. Your land needs your *connection*.'

'Connection?' repeated Jay.

'And Stitch needs your connection. Without you, Jay, your friend is vulnerable. The same as my counterpart – my level "C".'

Jay stole a glance at Stitch as he stared at the man, like he was trying to absorb the information. She turned back to the man. 'Why does the manipulator want Cassie?' said Jay.

'He wants *you*, Jay. Cassie is the bait. You are the 8C. Once he has you, the source and your Interland will be unprotected.'

The three fell silent, watching the ripples carve across the lake. The thought that she could be the target of the Readers and this manipulator sent fear running through Jay's veins once more.

The man spoke. 'There are three dead islands. Once the manipulator has you, Jay, your island will be the fourth.'

Dark clouds gathered above their heads, over the islands, reflecting the swirling blackness in the lake. 'But our Interland is safe,' said Jay. 'It's protected. There's Zadie, and all the level six and sevens.'

'What level is this manipulator, anyway?' asked Stitch.

'The manipulators no longer have levels. They were once part of the Given, but they rejected the power. The act of rejection generates a polar opposite reaction, a response in the energy that becomes as powerful – *more* powerful. The manipulator in this land, your land, we think, was a particularly powerful member of the Given before he rejected the power.'

Jay shook her head. 'Who is he? How did he reject his power?'

'We don't know. But a true and complete rejection of what is given brings the greatest of the reactive power – a darker power.'

Stitch crouched by the water, watching as the black swirls moved past the island. He reached out to touch the water. 'No,' screamed the man from the other side of the water.

But it was too late. Stitch had dipped his hand in the inky blackness. Steam rose from the water as Stitch screamed and withdrew his hand. The water bubbled, and the blackness intensified. Stitch rolled back onto the shore, his legs on the edge of the water, his foot dangling dangerously close to the expanding blackness. Jay lurched at him, pulling his leg away from the water. Stitch held his own wrist, his fingers burning, sizzling, the skin peeling back like the layers of an onion. He doubled over, retreating into a foetal position, holding on to his hand as if trying to stop it from disintegrating.

'What do I do?' Jay shouted over the water to the man, but he was gone. The white light came once more, and the islands dissolved into the fog. Stitch's whimpers turned to screams that reached such a volume Jay could do nothing but hold her ears.

Jay placed a hand on Stitch as he curled tighter. She felt hopeless and alone. The black swirls expanded and circled the island. Her heart raced, a thumping pain in her head distorting her vision. She closed her eyes and slowed her breathing. Elements of her world had slotted into place – releasing some of the tangles in her mind. The power, the source, and the connections with the environment went far beyond the boundaries of Jay's world. There was a bigger picture, a greater cause than personal freedom. The threat from the Readers was a threat to the very existence of the Given and the environment as they knew it.

Stitch lay motionless. Jay looked into the water at her own reflection in the gloss-black surface. She was alone. The girl in front of her looked spent and weak. Without Stitch, and without a connection between Nature and all the Given, she saw no hope for the resistance to the Readers, and the master manipulator lurking in the shadows.

PART III

19

Jay woke in the front seat of the car, her hands on the steering wheel. Samir was slumped in the passenger seat, eyes closed. Stitch leaned up against the back door, his cheek flattened against the window. The car's front end was submerged in the water of the lake. Jay leaned forward to look for islands, but there was nothing but water for as far as she could see, a light mist drifting across the lake's surface in the far distance.

She opened the door, lifting her feet to avoid the water gushing in to fill the driver's side footwell. Stitch stirred in the back, sitting to peer through to the front of the car.

'Your hand OK?' Jay asked.

'Feels weird.' Stitch and Jay exchanged a look. The skin on his hand was red, but seemed to cause Stitch no pain or discomfort. Without words, they acknowledged their shared experience. Stitch nudged his dad on the shoulder. 'Hey, wake up.'

Samir jolted awake, his eyes wide, streams of Arabic flowing from his lips. 'Dad,' Stitch tried to calm him, 'it's OK, we're OK.'

'What happened?' Samir said in English.

Jay and Stitch silently agreed to keep their experience to themselves for the time being. 'It's an old car, must have been a problem with the steering,' said Stitch.

Samir pushed open his door then recoiled at the sight of water flowing in, covering his feet. He grunted, speaking again in Arabic before stepping out into the water and wading the few feet to the shore. Jay and Stitch followed, the three of them standing on the shore looking at the car.

'If what we just experienced was real, then we need to get back to the Interland,' said Stitch. 'We can't protect the source from here.'

'Not before we get Cassie,' said Jay.

'You heard that man,' said Stitch, leaning close to Jay, fear in his eyes.

'What man?' said Samir.

Ignoring Samir, Jay said, 'We find Cassie first. Then we head back.' Jay turned back to the car and waded around to the driver's door.

'There'll be nothing to go back to if we don't leave now,' Stitch called after her. 'If he's right, the reason they have Cassie is to bait you, and me probably.'

'What man?' Samir repeated, his tone more urgent.

'I'm not leaving her there,' said Jay. Despite her fear, she knew in her heart that she wouldn't leave her friend.

Samir looked from Jay to his son and back again. 'What are you two talking about? Stitch?'

'Nothing,' said Jay. 'Stick to the plan.' She positioned herself to push the car up the shallow slope and onto the shore. 'You two going to help me get this car back on the road?'

Stitch splashed around to the front and Samir to the passenger door. With effort, they managed to roll the car backwards out of the lake, water pouring from the engine bay. Jay lifted the bonnet. 'See if she'll start,' she called to Stitch. He jumped into the driver's seat and turned the key. The starter motor whirred, and the engine turned but didn't start.

'There'll be water in the fuel,' said Samir, joining Jay at the front of the car. Jay leaned in and pumped the fuel supply hose a few times, then asked Stitch to try again. This time the engine caught and Stitch stepped on the accelerator to keep it ticking over.

20

Sammy barely touched his food. Instead, he watched as Zadie ate and spoke with her colleagues, their heads bowed, eyes furtive. Sammy's lack of trust for Zadie was matched only by his disdain for the two at her side. Both Simon and Jared were climbers, looking for attention and power. They'd do anything to get up into the realms of Zadie's world. As far as Sammy could remember, they were both at level six. Powerful enough, but always wanting more.

Pinto and Toyah sat with Sammy, listening intently to Alfred. He was their oracle, a mine of wisdom from his years as a bookseller and a double agent. There were few that knew more than Alfred about the inner workings of the State and the motives of the Readers.

'She looks harmless,' said Pinto, nodding towards the portrait of Sasha Colden on the wall above Zadie's head.

'Zadie?' said Alfred, knowing well enough that Pinto meant Sasha. Pinto laughed and Sammy saw the joy in Alfred's eyes at messing with Pinto. Alfred clearly adored Pinto, they had a special bond, and Alfred had said before he felt certain that Pinto had something strong developing, something unusual, a level-five. Toyah, at nineteen, had a clear number six on her wrist. Alfred always expressed surprise that her number wasn't higher, given the strength of the energy he could feel from her – but then, Alfred often exaggerated.

'She was far from harmless if you were a Reader,' Alfred said. 'Sasha Colden was lethal. Nothing touched her when she had her connected companion with her.'

'Who was her companion?' asked Pinto.

'Like Stitch, the level "C". We don't know who Sasha's level-C was, but we know they died, and Sasha lost something of her power too.'

Toyah pulled her sleeve back and scratched gently at her number six. Sammy watched as she studied it, turning away when she caught him looking. He shielded his thoughts. His shielding power was not strong, but enough to confuse. He looked again to see that Toyah had returned her attention to her wrist, a smile on her face and a hint of a blush on her face. For him? Sammy barely dared hope.

'You think I'll be a level eight, like Sasha, and Zadie, and like Jay?' asked Pinto.

Alfred slung an arm around his shoulder and pulled him close. 'My boy, I think it's possible. But, remember, it's not just the level eights that make this community tick. We need people at all levels to do the work if we are ever going to break free of the Readers.'

Sammy sighed, 'And I'm not convinced that Zadie is your best role model, Pinto.'

Alfred caught Sammy's eye, reading him. Sammy opened up, no longer wanting to hide his feelings about Zadie – her sneaking around, the sense that she was planning something, and her apparent mistrust of Jay and Stitch.

None of it quite added up for Sammy, and he needed someone to know, either to tell him to stop being paranoid, or to confirm his suspicions.

'She's under lot of pressure,' Alfred said, looking over towards Zadie. 'Much rests on her decisions in here.' Alfred's tone was not convincing. 'I must admit I preferred it when your sister was here,' he said. 'She certainly brought a sense of perspective and calm, gave Zadie someone to converse with about the powers, the strategy. Can't help but feel Zadie's a little less grounded here on her own.'

Sammy shuffled a little closer to Alfred. 'It's more than that. Can't you feel it?' he said, keeping his voice low. Toyah and Pinto looked over at Zadie, as if trying to see what Sammy was seeing. 'Don't stare,' said Sammy.

'What are you saying?' said Alfred, leaning forward, his arms resting on his knees. Sammy shrugged. He didn't know what he was saying. He had no evidence of anything to show that Zadie's intentions were anything but in support of the Given, and the protection of the Interland.

'It's just a feeling,' Sammy said. 'Maybe I'm wrong.'

Toyah huffed, 'If she's not on our side, we'd have been screwed a long time ago. She's the one that reaches out to the Given, brings them in. Me and Pinto wouldn't be here if it weren't for her.'

Sammy lowered his head. 'I found fertiliser and batteries in the store? What's all that for if not building bombs? What's she planning?'

'Have you communicated with Jay?' Alfred asked.

Sammy shook his head. 'I tried, at the source, but I couldn't get anything.' He was concerned for his sister. She wasn't confident when she left the Interland, and he knew that her vulnerability lay in her lack of self-belief. He sighed, recalling his last visit to the source that took him on a flight above the Interland – the Downs, the hill forts, and the darkness swirling through the valleys.

'You're not supposed to go down there, no one is,' said Pinto.

'*She* goes down there,' Sammy said, nodding towards Zadie, who was in deep conversation with Jared at her left-hand side. Zadie looked over towards Sammy, as if she could hear their conversation. He shielded. 'I saw her come up from there the other day,' he whispered.

'She's allowed. She's a level eight,' said Toyah.

As they watched, Zadie stood. Jared joined her and they motioned for Simon to follow. The three of them left the main cavern, heading out towards the exit, towards the waterfall beyond which was the one and only entrance to the caves. 'Where are they going?' asked Sammy.

Alfred watched after them. 'Secret liaison,' he said. Sammy exchanged a look with Alfred, only for Alfred to shake his head. 'Don't play with fire, Sammy.'

* * *

WITH SIMON AND JARED, Zadie stood just the other side of the waterfall that partitioned the underground – between the entrance zone, and the main caves and caverns of the Interland. Sammy crept as close to the waterfall as he dare, the three leaders talking in secret on the other side. He could hear nothing of their conversation for the noise of the water pouring from the rocks in the ceiling and away through the crevices in the floor.

After a few minutes, the three appeared through the waterfall. Sammy ducked out of sight, leaning back into an alcove in the rocks, hidden by the darkness. They passed him without hesitation. Zadie nodded at Jared and said,

'Collect your team. I'll see you back in the main cavern. Anyone who wants to join us, we welcome.'

'And if they don't come?'

'Then they're against the cause. We don't have time for opposition.' Sammy watched as Zadie locked eyes with Jared, communicating her instructions. Jared put a hand to his jacket pocket and his fingers closed over a gun. 'Like we discussed,' said Zadie. Jared nodded and slid the gun out of sight once more. Zadie looked at Simon. 'You come with me.'

Sammy remained still, not daring to move from the shadows, then jolted to attention at the sound of voices coming from the main cavern. Zadie was calling people together. He stumbled forward, picking his way through the darkness and into the light of the main cavern, now rammed with people. Mutterings of confusion grew louder as more squeezed into the room. Sammy raised himself up on tiptoes to see if he could locate the others. He caught sight of Toyah and pushed towards her. As he ducked between people, a shot rang out from deep in the caves, then another.

'Jared,' Sammy said under his breath, then refocused on moving quickly towards Toyah.

'Hush,' came the voice of Zadie Lawrence, perched on a rock so that she could see over the crowd that filled the room. Simon was by her side, and Sammy saw that he had a rifle in his hands. Back towards the entrance, Sammy noticed that Jared had reappeared, stood with three others, each with rifles. Looking to the waterfall, the route to the exit from the Interland, Sammy could see more of Zadie's soldiers, armed and fixed in position.

'Calm down, hear me out,' said Zadie, shouting above the background noise.

'Why are you holding us like this?' a man shouted.

'Who said I was holding you?' said Zadie, her powerful voice cutting through the noise. She pointed over to the main exit to the caves, where Sammy could see the waterfall in the distance. 'There is the exit. You are free to leave whenever you wish.' As she said the words, her soldiers at the exit to the cavern stepped aside to show that the exit was open. Sammy looked at their rifles, and the expressions on their faces. He wasn't convinced that they were preparing to let people do as they wished.

'We are entering a new phase of the work we have been doing down here, the work that was started by Sasha Colden herself,' she said. Sammy bristled at the sense that Zadie was using his grandmother to justify her plans. He moved a little further through the crowd towards his friends. Zadie continued, 'We have spent long enough hiding in the bowels of the earth. It's time we re-emerged into the world, to join those with power, not separate ourselves from them.'

Someone called out, 'We *are* together. The Given are mostly all here, safe from the Readers.'

Zadie hushed the crowd again as the noise level rose. 'We need to remove the threat, so that *all* those with power can unite. The Given, the Readers...' Noises of confusion and disagreement increased. 'Wait,' Zadie shouted. 'Think about it. What is it that tips the balance of power and sets people against each other? Reader against Given?' Sammy caught sight of Toyah and pushed through the final few metres of the crowd that separated them.

'Sammy,' she said, pulling him towards her and Pinto. Alfred stood at their side. He looked at Sammy and shook his head, his thoughts coming through loud and clear. Zadie was turning things around. She had a plan that he didn't yet understand.

Zadie stood tall now, shouting across the crowd. 'We need to re-establish the balance of power if we are to reach a steady state, without conflict, and without turning this into a full scale war that will destroy everything we are trying to protect. There's already been so much deterioration out there, even in the last twelve months. There are great parts of the country now run-down. Houses are empty. The economy is on its knees.'

'She's talking about joining with the Readers,' said Alfred.

'It's the segregation,' said Zadie. 'The imbalance that isolates the Interland from others with power – Given *and* Reader.'

'She wants to get rid of Jay,' said Sammy. He knew that the only thing that kept the Readers from being able to enter the Interland was its protection by the power of the 8C, and the connection – Jay and Stitch.

'Why?' asked Toyah.

It had crystallised for Sammy. 'Without Jay and Stitch, Zadie is the most powerful, and can allow access to the Interland to anyone she chooses, including the Readers.'

The background noise grew louder once more. 'Quiet!' Zadie shouted, then nodded towards Jared who pointed his gun back down the passageway and let off a round, the sharp noise echoing through the caves and silencing the crowd. 'Listen to me,' insisted Zadie. More shots rang out from the tunnels.

A fearful voice of a man called out from the crowd, 'What have you done? Where are the others? What have you done with the others?'

Sammy and Alfred exchanged a glance and then looked

back to Zadie, her expression neutral, her stance resolute. Sammy stretched to see over the heads of the crowd. 'Where's Dad?' he asked. Alfred shook his head.

The man shouted again, 'She'll destroy us.' He turned to the crowd. 'Can't you see?' A shot echoed through the cavern, fired at the wall by Zadie's other henchman, Simon. The dissenter froze. People screamed. Another shot at the floor near the man's feet this time. Then silence.

'I'm not asking for a consensus.' Zadie spoke slowly and deliberately. Someone interrupted but quickly quietened down as Simon raised his rifle once more and it was clear that Zadie had had enough discussion. 'These plans have been a long time in the making. We need to organise ourselves for the authorities. In a matter of hours, they will be here to help us repatriate the Given above ground.'

Noise grew once more until one of the crowd spoke in Zadie's defence. 'Listen to her. Has she not been here for us for all these months, years? Has she not looked after our interests for all this time? Don't you want to reintegrate above ground? We all have family up there, friends we left behind. We can't stay down here forever. This could be our opportunity for peace. Embrace it.' Zadie nodded, and the crowd quietened.

'We need to leave,' said Alfred, looking at each of the exits to the cavern.

'No chance. Too many of them,' said Toyah.

Pinto's voice shook as he said, 'They'll shoot us.'

Toyah put a hand on his shoulder. 'It won't come to that, we're getting out of here. Sammy, what about back through there?' She nodded towards the main exit, the waterfall.

'Too many of them,' said Sammy. He looked over his shoulder at the opening in the cavern that led through to the stores. Pinto caught his eye and Sammy nodded. 'The cold store has a connection through to the other passageways.'

'How do you know that?' said Toyah.

Sammy ignored Toyah's question and craned his neck to look for his dad. Still no sign of him. He edged backwards towards the unguarded entrance to the store. Alfred nodded at Toyah and Pinto to follow. 'I'll sit tight for a minute, make sure the coast is clear.' Sammy looked at Alfred, communicating his insistence that Alfred follow. Alfred nodded, and Sammy ducked into the storeroom.

The room was empty. As Toyah and Pinto followed him in, Sammy squeezed through the gap that led to the cool zone, the walls damp and noticeably cooler. He moved a sack of rice from the opening and waved Toyah and Pinto into the passageway. Alfred entered the room, his face etched with fear.

A guard held a rifle to Alfred's back. 'Move away,' he ordered.

As Sammy stepped aside, the man saw the opening. He moved towards it, rifle pointed towards Sammy. At the entrance, he ducked down and Alfred dropped an industrial tin of beans on the back of his head. The man went down, letting off a round from his rifle, the bullet pinging through the entrance to the passageway.

Alfred grabbed the motionless body of the guard and slid him away from the entrance to the tunnel, showing a strength that surprised Sammy. He waved Sammy through and followed him as they heard people approaching from the main cavern.

* * *

ZADIE PACED THE SMALL, rectangular room. She was buzzing still from the events in the main cavern. Her guards had retained control, and all but a few dissenters were on board – no longer resisting if not enthusiastically supporting. She had tried to get a message to Hinton that he would find the Interland as they had planned, with no resistance, so he needn't bring his entire army.

One of her guards, Simon, entered the room. 'No sign of them but those passageways go nowhere but down.'

'So they're out, they got out?'

'There is no way through to the outside, chances are they fell through to one of the shafts, and if that's the case they won't make it. They'll be at the bottom of a long drop to nothing but rock.'

'If Jay's brother is dead, then she'll know about it,' said Zadie, suddenly conscious that if Jay sensed it, she might change her strategy and return, instead of rescuing Cassie.

'What does it matter? She's not coming back here.'

'What about the father, Ben?'

'No sign. There are a number still unaccounted for. In the residential section.'

Zadie had assured Hinton the Interland would be clean by the time the Readers arrived. The Given would be out, and the Interland no longer a hidden base for conflict, but a place of peace, somewhere to be visited as a source of inspiration. The main connection into the underground would be sealed, leaving only the source accessible from the outside, nothing else. The source would become a place of pilgrimage for the Given, and a symbol of peace and progression for the Given and Readers alike.

'We can't set the fuse if there are people the other side of the wall,' said Simon.

'We follow the plan. We blow the connection tunnels when it's time.'

'They'll be locked in.'

'Just make sure that all those who are *with* us prepare to leave.' She waved the guard away, following him out of her room. She turned off the main path towards the passageway to the source.

Zadie lit three of the candles in the sub-level, taking a moment to admire the beauty of the flowing water, and the energy she felt emanating through the cave. With a hand in the source, the pool at the confluence of the three streams, Zadie sensed a presence.

'Davey?' she said aloud.

'I lost them on the road,' Davey replied. 'All three of them.'

'Three?'

'Jay, Stitch, and Stitch's father. Something happened at Stitch's house. The Readers closed in, but there was something else there, or someone, I don't know. The three of them got away from the Readers. I would have helped Jay and Stitch but it was all over so quickly. I followed them through to the main road up to the prison but their car ran off the road.'

'How?' Zadie asked.

'I don't know, it just veered off into the side, through the bushes. I parked up and searched, but there was no sign of them. The lake swallowed them up. Disappeared. But not dead. I can still feel them.'

'Where are you now?'

'Highdown. To see if I can get a sense of them. I have something. I think they're still on their way to the prison.'

'Things have changed here, Davey. We've lost some people. We need to abandon the Interland.'

'What? That makes no sense.'

'Not much here is making sense, but we have intelligence that Jay and Stitch might be behind the events here.'

'What events?'

'Readers.'

'Why...'

'No time to go through it all now. We can't let Jay go free and put the Interland at risk.'

'Shall I make contact?'

'No,' said Zadie. 'She's too powerful and we can't trust that she won't infiltrate and manipulate you. You need to stop her, you still have the rifle?'

Davey hesitated. 'It's on the bike.'

'Use it. Start with Jay. We can't afford to lose more ground.'

'But...'

'Then come back in, but not before it's done. If she gets to the Readers, we can't be sure what she'll do.' Zadie pulled her hand from the pool and took a breath. The communication with Davey ended.

Soon, with the support of the Readers, she would have control of the Interland. With no more of the Given at level 8C, it would be for her to drive change, a controlled reintegration of the Given back into society.

21

The car pulled into the parking area at the motorway services. The Little Chef restaurant was virtually empty.

'You take a seat, Dad. Me and Jay will order food.'

Samir found a table at the back, overlooking a patch of grass that led down to a wooded area away from the motorway. Jay and Stitch studied the laminated menu at the counter as the uniformed assistant waited just out of earshot.

'What happened back there?' Stitch said. 'Feels like it was all a dream.'

'It was real enough,' said Jay. She glanced at Stitch's hand. 'Looks sore.'

'More like a tingling sensation. It feels numb. Do you think the Interland could be taken? What about Sammy, and the others?'

'I can feel Sammy. Something's happening back there, but he's OK.' Sammy was almost always present in Jay's senses. Mostly he was the merest of feelings – a tingle in her temple. But sometimes his emotion came through in a rush, as clear as if he were in the same room.

'We need to get back...'

'Stitch,' Jay interrupted. 'We're not leaving without Cassie.'

Stitch shook his head. 'This whole thing is bigger than just us, just this.' He motioned around them.

'What do you mean?' asked Jay.

'The man said there are other Interlands, in other countries. They're choked, dying. Readers are closing in.'

'But...' Jay started.

'I know,' Stitch interrupted. 'I'm with you. We can't leave Cassie. I know that.' He paused for a moment, staring at the menu. 'But don't you think we're heading into a trap?' he said, looking up at Jay.

Jay nodded. 'Yes, I do. But if your dad knows a way in...'

The restaurant assistant appeared at the counter. She took their order of three cooked breakfasts, which Stitch paid for in cash.

Handing him his change, the woman said, 'You two Givens?'

Jay and Stitch exchanged a glance. As Jay was about to respond, Stitch got there first. 'No,' he said, his voice stiff.

'Thought I heard you sayin' so that's all.'

'Sorry, you must be mistaken,' repeated Stitch.

'We've had trouble before is all.'

'Trouble?' asked Jay.

'People had enough. Nothing but protesting and fighting. They think they're special. Think they're better than the rest of us. My husband, Jack, says we should've rounded 'em all up way back.' She lowered her voice. 'Now, I'm not so extreme as him, but he's got a point if you get my meaning?'

'What meaning?' asked Jay, bristling.

'Well, I ain't prejudiced or nothing like that, but this country was doin' just fine before, and now it's gone to shit. Used to be teeming with customers in here. Not anymore. No one got any money now.'

Stitch put the change into the tip-jar and pulled Jay away from the counter. 'We're with you on that,' Stitch said, giving Jay a look that told her to keep quiet. He shoved her into the booth next to Samir. 'Don't say anything,' he said. 'In case you haven't figured it out yet, the Given aren't so popular.'

'You're surprised?' Samir said, drawing quizzical looks from Jay and Stitch. 'You haven't been here, in the real world. The Given weren't popular even before you left. They're seen as the enemy now, by almost everyone.'

'Why?' said Stitch.

'People are scared. They believe what they read and see on TV...' Samir gesticulated wildly with his hands. 'They just want everything to get back to normal.' He sighed and looked out the window. 'Whatever *normal* is.'

The restaurant assistant approached with three plates, placing them on the table and sliding one across to Samir. She reached to the table next to them for cutlery and tomato sauce, asked if everything was alright, turned and left.

'Service with a smile,' said Stitch.

Jay picked at her fries. 'We met someone up at High-down yesterday,' she said to Samir. 'He told us that the Given have been driven underground.'

Samir choked a laugh. 'What's left of them. Most have been taken through rehab. Washed clean of their power, so they say on the television. The rest, if there are any who aren't holed up wherever you kids were, might be in hiding, or...' He trailed off, looking again out the window.

'Or what?' said Stitch.

'Or dead,' he said, not taking his eyes off the horizon.

22

Through the windscreen of the old Ford, the valleys stretched miles into the distance between the rolling hills of the Downs – occasionally punctuated with farms and villages that seemed to Jay untouched – something pure in the growing darkness of state oppression.

The landscape transformed as they crossed into the urban outskirts of Northtown, a once-affluent suburb of London. Its only distinguishing feature now was the ever-expanding prison, the rehabilitation centre that occupied more than half of the Northtown suburb.

Jay slowed as they entered the town. The day's light seemed to fade as they crossed the boundary. A fine rain hung like mist. The prison rose in the distance, austere and forbidding, the lights on its entrance pillars highlighting their rise. The car rolled to a stop next to the kerb.

'What?' said Stitch from the back of the car. Samir stirred in the front seat next to Jay, rubbing his eyes and then stroking his beard.

'It's too late to go in tonight,' said Jay. 'We need to find somewhere to stay.'

'They'll be looking out for us in town,' said Stitch. 'We can't just check in to a hotel.'

Samir sat up straight, peering through the gloom. 'Head to the east side, by the river.' Samir nodded towards a side road. 'There. Take that road down to the riverside and head east.'

'You know somewhere, Dad?' asked Stitch.

Samir sighed, looking out through the side window as Jay pulled the car back onto the road and indicated to turn right. 'Me and your mother lived over that side. When we first came over from Tripoli.' To Jay: 'Take a left here.'

Jay turned the car into a residential street, the Victorian townhouses neglected to the point of dilapidation. Windows on every other house were boarded, roofs of some collapsed and open to the elements.

'You lived here?' asked Stitch.

Samir shook his head. 'This was once the posh part of town.'

'Not anymore,' said Stitch.

'No one lives here now. I thought these houses might be intact enough for us to squat down for a night.'

There were no lights in any of the houses. The only cars parked in the street were blocked up on bricks, their wheels missing, windows smashed.

A shadow flashed across their path. Jay screeched to a halt. Stitch lurched forward, banging his head against the back of Samir's seat. Samir said something in Arabic, breathing rapidly. Stitch gathered himself in the back of the car. 'What was that?' he said.

'An animal, it's OK. A cat, probably,' said Jay.

'I don't like it here,' said Stitch, his voice thin and quiet.

'Look.' Samir pointed at one of the town houses. 'That one looks intact. Park the car and we can have a look.'

Jay parked between an old Transit van with its back door hanging off its hinges and a small white VW car that looked untouched. They collected their bags, making as little noise as possible so as not to alert anyone to their presence. A flash of light filled Jay's head, and she faltered, placing a hand on the car to steady herself. Another flash. A communication from someone using the power to reach her over distance. Sammy.

'You alright?' asked Stitch.

Jay nodded. 'Sammy's been trying to get a message to me. Let's get inside.' To Samir: 'Which house?'

Samir pointed. 'That one looks good.'

Jay and Stitch followed Samir through the alleyway at the side of the house and around to the back garden. The grass on the lawn was long. The shrubs around the perimeter had encroached on the neighbouring gardens, but Jay figured it hadn't been long deserted, a matter of weeks, not months.

Samir cupped his hands around his face and peered through the glass of the back door. 'Looks tidy,' he said. He tried the door handle. Locked. He looked under the doormat. Nothing.

'There's a cat-flap,' said Stitch.

Samir waved at Stitch to look. Stitch leaned down to thread his arm through the cat-flap to see if he could reach the lock from the inside. He squirmed and wriggled until eventually giving up and stepping away. He rifled through the bushes and came back with a stick. He tried again through the cat-flap. Jay heard a click and Stitch smiled, pulling his arm out and opening the door.

A waft of stale, damp air passed through the door as Jay stood in the threshold, Samir and Stitch behind her. She stepped into the kitchen, her ears hyper-sensitive to the slightest sound in the near silence that surrounded the house. If the Readers were looking out for them, or if they were following them, then this place would be the perfect location for an ambush. Out in the open, amongst the energy of the Downs, the sea and the environment, she could get a fix on the readers from some distance. It was different in the City.

'Go on then,' said Stitch.

Jay stepped over the threshold and into the house. A wave in the energy, a small fluctuation passed over Jay. Someone with power was nearby. She stopped and held up her hand to signal to Samir and Stitch to wait. The sense passed. Jay strained her eyes to see through the darkness in the kitchen and thought she saw a glimmer of light reflecting through the house from a distant room. The dark quiet was shattered when a scream pierced the silence.

A blunt object slammed the back of Jay's head. The pain was intense, but the blow was not so hard to knock her down. Before Samir and Stitch could get through the door, Jay turned to see the pale features of a man, arms raised. His eyes were wide, reflecting the light of the night sky, crazed and fearful. He gripped a baseball bat in his hands. Jay held up her hands in defence, but the man hesitated. In that split-second, Stitch launched himself through the door.

'Wait,' said Jay.

Stitch had the man's arms pinned to the lino floor of the kitchen, sitting on his chest to immobilise him and knocking the bat from his hand. 'Stitch,' Jay put a hand on his shoulder, 'ease off, please.'

Stitch relaxed his grip and edged himself away from the man so that the three of them stood over the prone figure, his eyes flitting from side to side as if seeking an escape route. 'Hey,' Jay said to get his attention. 'You have power, I can feel it.'

'You're not Readers,' the man said.

Jay shook her head.

The man sat up and Jay took a step towards him, crouching next to him.

'Jay,' said Stitch, urging caution.

'Are you alone in here?' Jay asked, looking around the gloom of the kitchen.

He nodded, struggling to his feet as Jay stepped back to allow him space. He moved to a wall cupboard and collected a bunch of candles, which he placed on the kitchen worktop before taking out a box of matches. In the light of the candles, Jay glimpsed his marking, a number one on his wrist. She could see that he was in his fifties or sixties. He'd not bothered to shave or cut his hair in a while. The bags under his eyes darkened in the shadows and the flicker of light from the candles.

'Sorry I hit you,' he said.

Jay rubbed the back of her head. 'I'd have hit me too, under the circumstances.'

He smiled and his face cracked, his eyes lighting up to reveal the younger version of the man underneath the weathered exterior. 'Why are you here? If you're not here for me, then what?'

'We're passing through,' said Stitch. 'We need somewhere to rest for the night.'

'Of all the empty houses you chose mine?'

'It was the only one with a full roof,' said Stitch.

Jay could see the man wasn't a threat. 'This is Stitch and his dad, Samir. And, I'm Jay.'

'My name is Sebastian.'

'Why are you here?' asked Jay.

Sebastian picked up one of the candles and blew out the others. 'Follow me,' he said. He led them to the middle room on the ground floor which had no windows looking over the street, or the back, just one that opened into the alleyway at the side. This room was Sebastian's home, with a bed along one side, and two sofas taking up much of the remaining space.

'What are you hiding from?' said Jay.

Sebastian sat on his bed and motioned towards the sofa. He pulled back his sleeve to show his marking. 'They're taking all of us now.' He nodded towards Jay's wrist. She edged back her sleeve.

'Oh no.' Sebastian sucked in air, staring at Jay's marking. 'Power that strong will be noticed. They'll detect you.' He stood, paced the room for a moment, and then sat back down on his bed. 'Why are you here? They'll sense you. You're the one they want. The rest of us are just a sideshow.'

'They won't sense me. I can shield.' Jay leaned forward in her seat. 'What do you mean they're taking all of us?'

'The last six months it's been a clean sweep. There are barely any Given left, and any that remain hide on the Downs, or they hole up somewhere like this.'

'Like Otis,' Stitch said.

'You can't stay here. They'll come.'

'One night,' said Stitch. 'We'll shield.'

Sebastian continued to pace, eyes moving rapidly from Jay to Stitch, then to Samir. 'One night. No more. You shield. If you get any sense of Readers, then you leave before you draw them in. You can use the upstairs. This is my space.'

Samir stood and turned to head upstairs. Stitch made to stand, but his dad held up a hand. 'I'll go.'

'Thanks,' said Jay to Sebastian. 'We'll be gone in the morning.' Jay felt another flash behind her eyes, like a migraine piercing her vision. 'Excuse me,' she said, and left the room.

Back in the darkness of the kitchen, Jay sat at the small table and cradled her head in her hands. The message was from Sammy. She allowed her mind to settle and decipher the signal. There was something happening back at the Interland, and someone was looking for Jay and Stitch, someone other than the Readers.

'What is it?' said Stitch, appearing in the doorway.

'Message from Sammy. Something's happened back there, and someone's tracking us.'

'Who?'

'That's all I got.' Jay shook her head.

Back in the middle room, Jay quizzed Sebastian about the events of the past few months outside of the Interland. Sebastian described how the tactics of the authorities had shifted from covert operations to all-out war against the Given. The public were being encouraged and when that didn't work, threatened to speak out if they know of anyone hiding from the State. People who sheltered the Given faced prison. The pretence of rehabilitation had been dropped. The fate of the Given was *reduction*, long-term imprisonment, or death.

'Someone told us there is a network,' said Jay. 'Links between the Given that remain on the outside?'

Sebastian snorted, 'Used to be. Not anymore. Like there used to be places we could meet without fear for our lives. If there are any others not yet reduced or killed, then it's news to me.'

'When's the last time you saw another of the Given?' said Jay.

'You're the first humans I've seen this close for nearly six months. That's the only reason I'm alive, and if you don't mind, I'd like to keep it that way. It'll be best for me if you're not here when I wake up tomorrow.' Sebastian pulled his bedcover over himself and turned away from Jay and Stitch. Stitch stood to leave, and Jay followed him up the stairs.

* * *

SAMIR HAD ARRANGED the beds so that he and Stitch could share the room. Jay glanced around the room for where to dump her bag. Samir caught Jay's eye and nodded towards the second set of stairs from the landing. 'Thought you'd be OK up in the loft. It looks comfortable up there. Make sure you close the curtains if you light any candles, we don't want to draw any attention.'

'Oh, OK. Thanks,' said Jay, deflated to be kicked out. 'So you were saying about the route into the prison complex? Via the sewer outfall?'

'When we lived here in Northtown,' Samir said. 'It was when they built the rehab centre. I mean, the prison. Most of the local community was people helping with construction.'

'Did you work on it? Or just Mum?' asked Stitch.

Samir shook his head. 'Your mother. I have no skills, you know this.' He smiled. 'Your mother was section project manager. She oversaw construction of the *education* wing.'

'I didn't know she did that,' said Stitch.

'She was a brilliant manager. Great with people. Brain like a big house, that woman. But the job made her sick. Asbestos. Silica. That place killed her and the State never took responsibility.' He paused a moment to gather himself. 'She knew a lot about how the place was built, how it was configured. There's something she told me that sticks in my mind which could be our way in.'

Stitch and Jay exchanged a look. 'Go on,' Jay said.

'Like I was saying in the car, the storm-water outfall from the whole of this area was built at the same time as the prison...'

'The what?' asked Stitch.

'The overflow tunnels that take storm water away and discharge it to the Thames. They only come into use during a major flood, like a once-in-a-hundred-year rainfall. The rest of the time they are mostly empty. And they are taking water from the prison camp.'

He continued, 'I think I know where we can find the connection outfall at the River. Then we just need to work our way back through the tunnels and into the prison complex. There will be surface water connections that we can use to get into the *education* wing.'

'How big are these tunnels? You can't go traipsing through sewers, Dad.'

'Could be two metres in diameter, big enough for walking, no problem.'

'Sounds perfect,' said Jay. 'But *you* need to stay here.'

'What-' said Samir.

'We need someone to see to the car and make sure it's ready for when we get back with Cassie.'

Samir looked at Stitch. 'What about you?'

'Jay will need me.'

'But what about...'

'Dad.' Stitch interrupted. 'Trust me. I'll be fine.'

Samir wore an expression of concern for his son. He shook his head and let out a sigh. 'I suppose I'm the only one who can get that car in shape. It needs a good flushing through of the fuel system since that dip in the lake.'

'Not here though,' said Jay.

Samir and Stitch looked at her. 'Where then?' said Stitch.

'There are some garages in the next street. I say we put the car in one of those. If someone comes for us, then you need to be somewhere out of sight.'

'What about Sebastian?'

'If we're not here, drawing them in, there's no reason to think the Readers will find him. Now, we rest. If we leave just before light, we can enter the storm-water tunnel while it's still dark?'

Stitch nodded, then looked at his dad. 'How far is it from here?'

'Twenty minutes' walk. I can make you a map. I don't know how many connections there will be at the river. One or two for sure, but maybe more. I suggest you take the first one and head north.'

Stitch looked at Jay. 'What do we do when we get into the prison?'

'We keep it simple. We go in quickly, pick up Cassie and straight back here, then back to the Interland. No messing around. I can sense Cassie from here, so when we get close, we'll know where she is.'

'Simple,' said Stitch.

JAY COULDN'T SLEEP. She was exhausted. Overtired and flushed with adrenaline. She stood and pulled back the curtain in the dormer window, looking over the streets of Northtown. It was not yet ten o'clock and she could see cars moving along the roads not far away. Some streets nearby remained occupied. She saw the lights of a pub just a few streets away and with her window open a little; she heard the waves of music coming over the rooftops on the wind. For a moment she craved the normality of an evening in a bar, a Guinness and some music – some time with friends without worrying about leaking her powers and attracting attention. She couldn't go to a pub, but she could at least get some fresh air.

She laced up her shoes and crept down the stairs, stopping for a moment at the door to Stitch and Samir's room where they slept in silence. She continued to the ground floor and leaned up against the open doorway to Sebastian's room. He looked up from his book. 'You leaving?'

'Just to get some air. Be back in a while.'

'Stick to the smaller streets. If the Readers are out patrolling, they'll be mainly on the central routes.'

'You should leave here, when we've gone,' said Jay.

Sebastian shook his head. 'I'm not moving again. This is it for me. If they catch up with me here, then it's meant to be. I can't keep moving, not at my age.'

Jay laughed. 'You're not old.'

'Feel it. Comes a point when you have to stop running.'

'I'm beginning to see that,' said Jay, turning to head for the back door. She paused. 'Thanks,' she said. 'For putting us up.'

'Whatever it is you're doing tomorrow, I hope you succeed. And I hope that this situation can be brought to an end sometime soon.' They locked eyes for a moment and Jay sensed that Sebastian was urging her on, to take action beyond that for herself and her friends. The whole of the Given were little more than a residual underclass hiding out in city squats and rural camps, waiting for their time to come at the hands of the Readers.

A fine rain dampened her face, and she dabbed her eyes with her sleeve. She pulled up her hood and headed out to the street. In her solitude, in the open air, a sense of freedom ran thorough her veins like she hadn't felt since she first entered the Interland.

A motorbike roared in the distance, getting closer. She turned down an alleyway and picked up speed, turning another corner before she heard the motorbike pass by out of sight. Her heart slowed once more, and she kicked herself for straying too far, for not being careful for Cassie's sake as much as her own.

At the end of the alley, the grey-black surface of the river was ruffled by a blustery wind. She crossed the road and leaned over the railing, looking down at the river wall to see if she could locate the storm-water outfall Samir had spoken of. It was too dark. She could see nothing but the blackness of the river wall in shadow. As she lifted her head, the wind caught her hood and blew it back onto her shoulders, exposing her ears. A loud crack made her jump, its echo bouncing off a building in the distance. She pulled up her hood and tilted her head to listen. Nothing but the wind.

avey opened up the throttle of his motorbike and screamed along the river road and into position. He wore his rifle strapped across his back. He'd seen Jay go into the alleyway by the river. She only had one possible destination. If he could get to the river first, he'd be able to find a spot out of sight. He'd be close enough for his rifle in the wind and poor visibility, and far enough away that he could escape without being seen.

Zadie's instructions echoed in his head. It made no sense to Davey. Why kill the most powerful of the Given? There could be no reason for Jay to succumb to the powers of the Readers. She prevailed in the face of great power from Readers before, surely she would not be so easily overcome. But Zadie would have intelligence that he was not party to, so who was he to question?

He stopped by the river and pushed his bike out of sight behind a disused block of garages. Taking shelter from the misty rain under a lean-to, he took the rifle out of its bag. He wiped the rain from his face and strained to see through blurred vision to load four bullets into the barrel. He clicked it shut and wiped the moisture from it before lifting it to his shoulder to take aim. He focused the crosshairs at space at the end of the alleyway where he expected Jay to appear at any moment. Satisfied that he was close enough for a clean shot, he lowered the gun and waited.

As he waited, he daydreamed. With Jay dead, Zadie would consider him worthy of higher-level duties. He would have demonstrated his loyalty, and his effectiveness. She would surely choose him to lead with her when the Given emerge from the Interland.

Jay appeared at the end of the alleyway, as Davey had predicted. His nerves tingled as he raised the rifle to his shoulder, his cheek against the cold metal. He held Jay in the crosshairs as she walked across the road, her hood down and hair blowing in the wind. He watched as she wiped the rain from her face and leaned up against the railing, peering over at the water. In the telescopic sights, he could see her expression, the searching look in her eye.

He removed the safety and maintained his aim. Jay leaned further over the railing and continued to scan the water's edge, her hood now falling so that it covered her head once more. Davey had the most powerful of the Given in his sights, the one for whom the whole of the Interland had been waiting for so long. The one who had the potential to raise the chances of the Given to match the power of the State.

His finger pressed on the trigger.

He inhaled slowly and held his breath.

The wind died.

He couldn't do it.

Something heavy hit him from the side and he thought he'd been hit by a car, the force was so great. His rifle released a shot as he went down, the bullet pinging harmlessly off the concrete of the garage and into the darkness behind him. Its noise swept away with the wind. He scraped his face along the asphalt floor, pain swallowing him and obscuring his vision. His face was slammed into a puddle on the floor so that his mouth and nose were under water. He tried to scream, tried to shift the sudden, heavy weight from his back. The thing had his head in a solid grip. With one final push, Davey turned his body and dislodged his assailant from his back, sending him to the ground. He was a small man, and Davey was surprised at how much force he'd been able to muster in taking Davey out. They both stood, Davey wobbly on his feet like a newborn lamb, a mix of rainwater and blood stinging his eyes and blurring his vision.

His assailant kept his distance. He was a good foot shorter than Davey, stocky with a beard and straggly hair. In the blink of Davey's eye, his attacker had covered the distance between them and again powered into him at waist level, taking Davey to the floor. Davey hit the ground hard, landing on his back, winded. The long-haired man sat astride him and let loose a shower of punches. This man was quick, but he was no fighter. Davey fought back, bucking the man off his chest and back onto the floor. They both scrambled to their feet, but Davey was ready this time. He assumed a boxing stance and kept a distance. Twice the man ran at him, and twice he dodged and landed blows to the back of his head as he passed.

Keeping his arms up to protect himself, Davey led with his left and landed a powerful right, then a left to the chin. He stumbled but kept upright, running at Davey once more, this time making contact so that they both went down.

They rolled and scrabbled on the ground, the hairy man having more success from close quarters until Davey pushed him away and released two powerful blows. He came again, his energy relentless, landing his own blows with his fists to Davey's jaw, cheek, eye.

Davey was exhausted, in agony, and seeing double. Both men bled from cuts on their faces, above their eyes, their lips. He landed a good punch on the man's nose, rocking him back on his heels, then took a punch himself on his left eye, which already gushed blood.

'What do you want?' screamed Davey through the noise of the pouring rain and the pounding of his pulse in his ears. 'Why are you doing this?' he trailed off as he gasped for breath, his arms heavy at his sides.

The hairy man stepped back and leaned up against the wall. Davey was relieved that he seemed just as exhausted, and just as willing to stop, at least for a moment. The man nodded towards the rifle on the floor. 'That's why.'

'You're a Reader?' Davey said, knowing that this man was no Reader. If he was, then Davey could tell for sure. He could sense power, but not that of a Reader.

The man shook his head. 'Why would I stop you killing a Given if I were a Reader?' He paused, holding his ribs and struggling to get air into his lungs.

'I wasn't going to shoot,' said Davey. The man snorted a laugh and Davey said, 'I changed my mind.'

'Why are you here, tracking and holding a gun at Jay Macfarlane?'

Davey remained silent for a moment, contemplating the sense in telling this stranger why he was pointing a gun at Jay. Although he'd changed his mind, for good reason, he retained a loyalty to Zadie, and to the cause.

'You changed your mind, so I assume you've come around and seen sense?'

'Orders,' said Davey.

'Whose?' asked the man.

'Doesn't matter. I changed my mind, like I said. What do you care?'

'There aren't many of us left. It's up to all of us to care if we want to survive the Readers, and people like you.'

Davey straightened, finally breathing normally again. 'Look, I was told that she was turning to the side of the Readers...'

'You're crazy.' The man picked up the rifle and emptied it of bullets before throwing it into the river.

'Maybe.' Davey looked across the road where light emitted from the ground-floor windows of a pub. 'What do you say we get dry?' He nodded towards the pub.

The man hesitated a moment, looking Davey up and down. 'OK,' he said. 'Let's drink.'

Davey collected his motorbike and pushed it behind the man, picking up speed to catch him. 'I'm Davey,' he said.

The man looked back at Davey, choosing not to reply.

THE BARMAN PLACED two pints on the table. The men had edged as close as they could bear to the open fire, steam rising from their wet clothes. He said his name was Otis. In the light of the pub, Davey could see that he was younger than he'd thought, perhaps as young as him. They remained silent as they peeled off their outer layers and draped them over chairs by the fire.

The landlady of the pub approached with a first aid kit from behind the bar. 'You boys had some trouble?' she said.

Otis nodded. 'We saw them off.'

She took a seat next to Otis and inspected his wounds. 'Nothing permanent by the looks of it.' She used a sterile wipe to clean him up and applied two steri-strips to the gash above his eye before turning to Davey.

'Thanks, you don't have to...' said Davey.

'We look after our own,' she said, pulling back her sleeve to show Davey a number-three in a deep black marking. She nodded toward his wrist, where his own number was hidden by his sleeve. Otis looked startled. Davey simply nodded and sat back to allow her to clean him up. He presented a more difficult task than Otis by virtue of the gravel-graze up the whole of one side of his face.

'I'm Otis. This is Davey,' Otis said as the landlady patched up Davey's cuts and scrapes. 'How did you know?'

'Sandy,' said the landlady. 'And that there behind the bar is Bill. Power can sense power.'

'I didn't sense any power in here before we came in,' said Otis.

Sandy glanced at him. 'Why do you think we're still here? You won't see many of the Given in plain sight unless they're particularly skilled at shielding, like me and Bill are.'

'That explains it,' said Otis.

Otis lifted his sleeve to show the number five. Davey hadn't seen a level five before. There were none inside the Interland. Plenty of fours, and a fair few at level six. Then there were all the Runners at level seven, like him. He guessed Otis might have something of the power he'd not seen before.

The barman, Bill, dimmed the lights and locked the doors as the other lone customer in the place walked out.

'You closing up?' asked Otis.

'Not to you,' said Sandy. 'You rest up, get dry. Bill will get you something to eat.'

Sandy left them to their drinks, and Otis eyed Davey. 'What?' said Davey.

'You were going to tell me why you were taking aim at the one chance the Given have of standing up to the Readers.' Davey looked away, took a drink from his pint. Otis continued: 'I'd feel a lot more comfortable if you handed over your weapons.'

Davey reached for his bag and pushed it over towards Otis. He considered for a moment how he must appear to Otis. Otis wouldn't know that Davey could never have taken that shot. As much as he supported Zadie Lawrence, her cause, the fight for the re-integration of the Given, he was sure that killing Jay was not the way to do it. 'How did you know I was there?'

'I've been tracking them since Highdown,' said Otis. 'Saw you up there too, spying on them.'

'You have wheels? A car?'

'Little moped. Enough to keep up.' Otis looked almost embarrassed. 'I kept back a bit, to see what you were up to. Good job I did.'

Davey sighed, 'I told you, I changed my mind, I wouldn't have taken the shot.'

'So you say.'

'Why are *you* following them?' asked Davey. 'Why aren't you *with* them?'

Otis leaned forward in his seat, grimacing at pain emanating from somewhere in his body. He warmed his hands on the fire. 'We met, but she doesn't trust me yet.'

'Why not?'

'Just cautious. Quite right too, given what you just tried to do.' He paused, trying to catch Davey's eye. 'I can help them. They just don't know they need it.' Otis stood with his empty glass. 'Another?'

Bill placed two bulging plates of pie and chips on the

table. 'On the house,' he said, walking away before Davey had a chance to thank him.

Otis placed the drinks down and snatched up his plate of food. 'You were going to tell me about your apparent assassination instructions?' He spoke through a mouthful of chips.

'Zadie Lawrence,' said Davey, picking up his own plate of food and resting back in his armchair.

Otis stopped mid-chew. '*She* issued the order to kill Jay?' Davey nodded. 'What for?' said Otis.

Davey shrugged. 'Like I said. Jay's under suspicion.'

Otis shook his head as he ate. 'No. Something's gone wrong. I could feel it, but didn't for a minute think it was Zadie Lawrence. That puts a different complexion on things.'

'What things?' said Davey. He was curious that Otis knew of Zadie Lawrence.

'Everything has been deteriorating for the Given over the last six months. The State has stepped up its campaign, forcing us into hiding. The Interland seemed more and more of a myth. With no one coming out of there to support the Given, people assumed it was a fabrication.'

'And you?' said Davey.

'I have a stronger sense for the Given and the powers than most. I could feel it. But the other connections between those on the outside have weakened so much that the Given might as well not exist out here. Then I saw those Runners.'

'Cassie and Reuben,' said Davey.

'The Readers closed in on them,' Otis continued, 'and flushed out Jay, the last of the big powers of the Given.'

'You think this was planned by the Readers?'

'With Jay under their control, there's nothing to stop the Readers putting an end to the Interland, and to the Given.'

'Except Zadie Lawrence and all the rest of the Given back at the Interland. She's a level-eight, remember.'

'Zadie Lawrence?'

'Yes,' said Davey

'The one who issued the order to take out Jay?'

'What benefit can she possibly get from destroying her own kind?'

Otis took a slug of his drink and shook his head. 'That's what we still have to find out. We need to get to Jay and Stitch, to convince them that there's something going on back at the Interland, persuade them to return.' Otis paused. 'That is, if you're with us, and not against us?'

Davey held Otis's eye. He was as sure as he'd ever been of what side he was on. Zadie had used him for her own twisted plans. He just didn't know why. Jay and Stitch were heading to save their friend, and walking right in to a trap. 'I'm with you,' Davey said, and they chinked their glasses together.

24

Sammy froze as an explosion shook the surrounding ground. A few stones fell from the roof of the tunnel. In the light from his torch, Sammy watched as the colour drained from Alfred's face.

Pinto held on to Toyah's arm, squeezing tight as they waited. 'What was that?' asked Toyah.

Sammy shone his torch into the blackness ahead of them. 'They were using fertiliser to make explosives. They're bringing the place down.'

'Why?' asked Pinto.

Alfred sighed, and the others looked at him. 'She's blocking off connection with the deep Interland.'

'But why?' Pinto said again.

'Control,' said Sammy. 'She's all about control and power. I can feel it now.'

Alfred turned on his own torch and pointed it up ahead through the gloom. 'Where does this lead, Sammy?'

'To the connection.' He explained how the opening in the roof of the tunnel near his room led to a series of passageways that eventually led back to where they were.

'So we can get to this place from here, the Free Cave?' said Alfred.

Toyah shuffled closer to Alfred. 'But then what? We can't get back to the main cavern and out through the waterfall. If we are going to get out of here, we need to get back to the exit. That way.' She nodded back towards the store, back the way they had come.

'We can't go back that way,' said Pinto, his voice quivering a little.

'Pinto's right...' Sammy started before he was interrupted by another explosion. This time the noise came from behind them, back through the tunnel.

'That settles it,' said Alf. 'They've blown the entrance. Only way is forward.'

Sammy looked at Toyah. 'The ledge,' he said.

She nodded.

'Follow me,' said Sammy, and he surged ahead.

AT THE CONNECTION, Pinto automatically took the right branch before Sammy called him back. 'Left,' said Sammy.

'It's always right,' said Pinto, turning back towards Sammy.

'Not from this direction, look.' He pointed his torch down the left branch to show Pinto the familiar tunnel bending around towards where they'd find the slope down into the Free Cave. Pinto recognised it and led the way. At the top of the slope, Sammy and Pinto turned to Alfred. 'It's not as bad as it looks,' said Sammy.

'This isn't for an old man,' said Alfred, a pained expression.

'We can go together,' said Toyah, stepping forward and

linking her arm with Alfred. He smiled at her and she showed him how to position himself, then edged him forward alongside her and they slid down together.

'Me next,' said Pinto. Sammy followed.

At the cave, Toyah and Alfred were already heading for the rock face that led up to the high ledge. Sammy knew that this was their best hope of a route out of the underground. When he and Toyah explored the ledge before, he could see that the tunnel led down and away from the caves. If it continued in that direction, it might lead all the way through to the south edge of the Interland.

Or it might lead to a sheer drop, broken bones and a bottomless pit from which they'd never escape. They knew nothing about the nature of the caves and openings in the rocks between the Free Cave and the outside. They didn't even know if there was a route to the outside. They could be trapped forever. But they could do nothing else but try. Sammy thought of his dad, hoping he'd got himself on the cavern side of the blockage.

Alfred and Toyah were the first to make it up onto the ledge, each helping the other along the way. Pinto wasn't far behind. Sammy eventually pulled himself up. Sammy edged the group forwards through the tunnels. Water seeped through the walls and roof. In some places it poured through cracks and flowed through the tunnel under their feet. In these sections, the air was cool and fresh. In other sections the tunnels were dry, and the air stale.

There could come a time when the air would run out and they'd be walking into their grave, gradually overcome by carbon dioxide and slipping into unconsciousness.

As the cave widened a little, Pinto caught up with Sammy to walk alongside him. 'What about the others?' he said.

Sammy pushed away the thought that his dad might have been caught the wrong side of Zadie's explosion. He and his dad had drifted apart a little since being on the inside. As much as Sammy refused to accept that it had anything to do with the revelation that Ben wasn't his biological father, he knew that was part of it. Ben was the only father he'd ever known. His biological father, Marcus, was nothing to him – a Reader destroyed by Jay. Ben was a good man in Sammy's eyes, even if the connection between them had become strained.

The cave narrowed. Toyah and Alfred separated as they negotiated tight opening after tight opening. Alfred slipped sideways through a gap, followed by Toyah, then Pinto and Sammy. On the other side, the cave opened in two separate directions. The simplest, widest path was to the right, but Sammy sensed the left branch was the one. It was the left path through which the water flowed. The water must know which way to go to get out. 'This way,' he said.

Toyah snorted, 'You're kidding?'

'He's right,' said Alfred, moving in to take the lead. He lay down to squeeze beneath the wedge of rock that formed their ceiling and scraped himself through. Toyah followed, and Sammy next – Pinto last. The other side, the cave narrowed further and Sammy couldn't move his arms. He squeezed along the thin passage by shuffling his back and arm muscles like a worm. Alfred and Toyah were quicker than Sammy, putting a distance between them. Pinto stayed with Sammy, nudging up against him. Sammy's thoughts swam darkly around his head. No one would ever find them in this dark place, hundreds of feet below the surface, if one of them were stuck or crushed.

Alfred called back, 'Big drop coming up. It's tight, you need to go through sideways.'

Sammy hesitated, looking back past Pinto in the direction they'd come. 'What's the matter?' said Pinto, looking around.

'Nothing,' said Sammy. Fear pulsated through every cell in his body. He'd never felt claustrophobic before, hardly batted an eyelid at the caving that he'd done since being in the Interland, but now the walls were closing in. Turning back wasn't an option. They were winding deeper underground, in pitch darkness, possibly trapping themselves. They had no choice but to press on and hope.

Alfred shouted through the gaps in the rocks up ahead. Alfred's voice. Sammy's skin prickled and his heart raced. He strained to see in the complete blackness beyond the torchlight. Push forward. His body swelled in his panic, filling the space between the rocks so that he became wedged. He talked himself down in his head, told himself to relax, breathe, move slowly. Another shout from Alfred, this time a noticeable hint of pain in his voice.

'My hands are slipping,' Alfred called. Sammy could move again. He could see Toyah now, leaning and reaching through the rock towards an opening in the floor, then adjusting her position and pushing herself further through.

'Toyah!' called Sammy.

'What is it?' Pinto's voice was taught.

Alfred shouted again, 'I'm slipping.'

'Nearly there,' Toyah said, but as Sammy reached her he saw over the ledge that Toyah was nowhere near him. Alfred hung on to a ledge more than fifteen feet below them. If his hands slipped, the drop was at least another twenty feet.

'I can jump,' Toyah said.

'You're joking,' said Sammy as he pushed himself over the ledge to reach for Alfred. 'You'll break your legs jumping that far.'

'If he falls, he'll die.'

'Let *me* go,' said Sammy. But, as Sammy readied himself to climb down to reach Alfred, one of Alfred's hands slipped off the ledge and he swung wildly out into the opening. Before Sammy could react, Toyah flew past him and landed on the ledge, reaching out for Alfred.

Toyah landed hard on the rocks, her arm outstretched to Alfred, a lifeline for him to pull himself up to safety. 'Toyah!' Sammy called, seeing that she'd knocked the back of her head. There was desperation in his voice as he repeated her name and scrambled down the rest of the well they'd found themselves in.

Sammy pulled Toyah's now unresponsive body back further onto the ledge as Alfred climbed back up with Pinto's help. Sammy laid Toyah on her back, feeling around her head for any obvious wounds. His hand came away bloodied. He called her name, trying not to let panic come through in his voice. Alfred sat back against the rocks, breathing heavily. 'I'm sorry,' he said.

Pinto moved towards his sister, his eyes glazed over. Sammy shook Toyah a little more vigorously.

Pinto leaned over her. 'She's dead,' he said.

'No,' said Sammy. 'She's unconscious, but she's alive.'

'She's dead,' Pinto repeated, hysteria building.

Sammy took Pinto by the shoulders and looked into his eyes. 'She's OK.'

Pinto seemed to come around. He calmed down. He leaned over his sister to confirm her breathing. Sammy felt useless. Responsible. This was his idea. He was the one who directed them through the caves. He could have led them out of the Interland with Zadie, and with everyone else. This was all his fault. He thought of Jay, and of his dad. What would they do?

Sammy watched in awe as eight-year-old Pinto deployed his training received in the medical centre. He was calm, as if in autopilot. He made sure that Toyah was comfortable, laying his jacket over her, then turned to Alfred. 'You OK?'

'My ankle,' said Alfred, his breathing in shallow bursts as he tried to control the pain.

'Could be broken,' Pinto said. 'When we move again, we'll have to help him keep the weight off it.'

'*Move* again?' Sammy said. 'Are you kidding? We're not going anywhere like this.'

'Sammy.' Alfred raised his voice and Sammy sat back against the rocks. He watched as Toyah's chest moved up and down with her breathing. He willed her eyes to open and for her to sit up, rub the back of her head and make some stupid comment. But moment after moment passed, and she didn't wake.

25

S unlight poured into Jay's room. For a moment she thought she was back in the loft bedroom of her childhood home on Beach Lane. It was just over a year since she had last woken in that room, but it felt like a lifetime. She was a different person, and it was a different world.

She'd slept well past their planned departure. She dressed quickly, her clothes still damp from the previous night. Stitch and Samir were awake, readying themselves to leave. 'Hurry,' said Jay, continuing down the stairs, past Sebastian's closed door and into the kitchen. She checked the cupboards. Mostly tinned food. She found a box of cereal and poured some into a bowl, eating the dry wheat flakes with her fingers.

Stitch entered the kitchen and picked a bowl from the cupboard, following Jay's lead with the dry cereal. 'You look like shit,' he said.

'Couldn't sleep for the snoring coming from your room.'

Stitch rolled his eyes. 'Look,' he said, showing Jay his hand, flexing his fingers. The redness had gone.

'Looks better.'

'I did some work on it last night,' said Stitch.

'Your healing trick?'

Stitch smiled, pride pouring from him. 'It's not a trick. I'm getting better at it. There's something in the way I align my thoughts and channel the energy. It's difficult to explain.'

'I'm impressed. Your dad OK?'

'It's been weirdly good to spend some time with him,' said Stitch. 'He's been talking about Mum this morning. First time he's spoken about her like this since she died. It's like he's finally getting his head above the water and seeing that there's a world out there.'

'Ironic,' said Jay.

Stitch nodded. 'Seems everywhere we go there are people squeezed by the State, living in deprivation and terrified of Readers. The only Given still out here are the ones who have learned to shield and avoid detection,' he said. 'And everyone else seems to have had enough, happy to see the end of the Given if that means peace.'

'The State are weeding the Given out of society. They're blaming them for the unrest and the economic downturn. So then the State becomes more powerful. People must realise what's happening,' said Jay.

'How many of the Given do you think have been lost in these purges?'

Jay shrugged and shook her head as she pushed the cereal around her bowl with her finger. She'd not yet allowed herself to think about it in terms of numbers. Her dad, Ben, had told her before that around one in a thousand people had some level of power, though the higher power levels were rare. That would make around sixty thousand Given in the UK alone. There was no way of knowing how many of those were in hiding, and how many had been taken through rehabilitation. Some would have passed through rehab and would now be powerless. Others would have died in the process, either through becoming reduced too far to sustain life, or through their own resistance to the reduction – and the rest would now be Readers.

'What's that?' said Stitch, taking Jay's hand and examining a graze she'd got back at Samir's house. His hands were warm, his touch gentle.

'Just a scratch,' said Jay, allowing Stitch to cradle her hand for a moment.

Samir entered the kitchen, and Jay yanked her hand back. Stitch turned to his dad, who was munching on a pastry. Stitch looked from his bowl of dry cereal to his dad. 'Where did you get that?'

'Sebastian gave it to me. He's got a whole load in there.'

Stitch snorted and pushed his bowl away.

'Let's go,' said Jay. To Samir: 'I'll show you the garages on the way out, then you can get the car?'

Sebastian came into the kitchen, holding out a torch, which Jay took with a nod of thanks. 'God speed,' he said.

THE TIDE WAS OUT, revealing a strip of mucky sand and gravel at the water's edge from which Jay looked up at the circular opening in the river wall. Water dribbled from its rim and down the wall, a stain only visible from the riverside. The opening was at least twenty feet above their heads, and there was nothing to indicate whether it would lead them to the prison. A column of step-irons led up to the grill fixed to the opening.

Stitch had to jump to reach the first step-iron. He missed and fell back down. At the second attempt he got a grip and with his foot found a ledge from which to push himself up to the next hand-hold. He looked over his shoulder and nodded for Jay to follow.

Stitch reached the opening as Jay was still halfway up the wall. As she reached the level of Stitch's feet, she heard a scrape and a crack as he pulled the grill free, holding on to it for long enough to launch it beyond Jay and down to the shore. Water and sludge spurted out of the hole, and Jay leaned away to avoid the spatter. Stitch pulled himself up and into the hole, standing without the need to duck his head. Jay climbed the final few metres and joined him, rejecting his offer of a hand and pulling herself up next to him. They looked out over the river for a moment before turning to head into the darkness.

Jay used the torch to illuminate the invert of the tunnel, dry but for a trickle of water, and mostly clean. She had a sense of the direction to the prison. The further they walked, the stronger Jay's sense of pull towards Cassie, and towards a body of power that was the collective energy of the Given incarcerated at the prison. Without having to articulate it, she knew that Stitch also sensed they were heading in the right direction. Only twice did Jay have to pause for more than a moment at an intersection between tunnels, where the signal was ambiguous. On both occasions, Stitch knew which way to go.

A loud clank echoed through the tunnels from behind them, as if someone had dropped a hammer. Jay looked at Stitch and they peered into the darkness. They held their breath, something scuttled from somewhere to their left. 'Rats,' said Stitch.

'Rats don't make that kind of clunking noise.'

'Let's go.'

After about an hour of walking, they came to the base of

a circular concrete-lined shaft that stretched above their heads for thirty feet to the open air through a steel mesh. Water dripped from above, both from the mesh at the top and from several connections to the shaft from smaller pipes at different levels. Jay could see that there was a metal hatch in the mesh that would allow them to get through and out to the surface. Step-irons ran all the way up from where they stood. Jay took the lead this time, steadily climbing towards the hatch at the top, the air growing cooler and fresher as she climbed.

At the surface, Jay edged up the hatch with her head and scanned the yard for signs of guards. Nothing. They rolled out onto the grass and without a word; they made a dash to the cover of the main building, stopping and crouching by a wall. 'She's close,' said Jay, her voice barely a whisper. 'Follow me.'

'Wait!' Stitch said, nodding towards a building on the other side of the yard. Three men walked around the corner of the building and made their way towards the front entrance. 'Readers?'

'Feels like it,' said Jay as the men disappeared into the building.

Stitch followed as Jay stalked between the low-rise buildings towards the main prison block. As they edged around the last of the low-rise, the vast expanse of the back wall of the prison façade came into view. A short dash across the yard and they'd be at the doors in the centre of the block. No sign of any guards, but the building façade was littered with windows from which they might easily be seen. Stitch followed Jay's eyes and scanned the windows for signs of life. 'Can't see anyone.'

They made a run for the doors. They rested a moment in the doorway as Jay looked back over the yard, eyes alert to any movement. Nothing. 'Weirdly quiet,' she said to Stitch. 'This is too easy.'

'Don't knock it,' Stitch said as he turned and pushed the door which swung open to the corridor beyond. It reminded Jay of a school corridor, running almost as far as she could see, doors off to each side. Deserted. Stitch pressed on and Jay told him to slow down so that she could get her bearings. Her senses told her that Cassie was on the ground floor, on the other side of the building.

From a side corridor, two figures appeared. They stopped in front of Jay and Stitch, in a stunned silence.

Jay knew immediately that the two men were Readers.

She sensed their confusion at Jay and Stitch's presence. She took advantage of their hesitation. She and Stitch connected and combined their power to attack the Readers simultaneously.

Jay felt a wave of energy from them, an attack of their own, but it was quickly overcome by the far stronger combined power of Jay and Stitch. Both Readers fell to their knees, each with his hands raised to the sides of his head. Jay continued to push her energy into their minds, reducing them until they flopped to the floor.

Stitch crouched next to the nearest Reader. He was unconscious, a scar forming on the side of his face.

'More?' Jay tensed, ready to continue the attack, to be sure that they wouldn't come back at them.

Stitch raised a hand to signal for Jay to stop. 'Enough. They're out.'

Jay relaxed. She breathed again. 'Let's move before more of them arrive.'

As they reached halfway along the corridor, the space opened out into a circular, double-height atrium, ringed by a series of steel doorways. They backed up against the wall

and looked up into the higher levels, scanning for movement. They communicated without talking.

No sign of any more Readers.

A sense of Cassie.

An uneasy feeling.

Stay alert. Be quick.

Jay remained still. Energy flowed at her in waves from
beneath her feet - a dark energy that left a bitter taste in her
mouth. The power of the Given was weak within the circle,
and Jay felt vulnerable. She itched to get out as quickly as
possible. Stitch walked away from her, circling the perimeter, his hand brushing the surface of each door as if trying to
feel for Cassie. Jay was certain that their friend was behind
one of these doors. She approached the nearest door, a
heavy, steel structure. A panel next to the door was open.
She peered inside to see a control board with a series of
buttons, and a blank screen.

Jay caught sight of something across the room. She
turned to see that a man had appeared beside Stitch. Her
heart raced. Her feet frozen to the spot.

Stitch turned to the man, then took a step back, looking
up into his face. Jay sensed that this man was not a Reader.
He had no power.

She wrenched her feet from the floor and made around
the perimeter towards them. She tried to read him but got
nothing. She pushed her influence into his mind but faced a
resistance she'd not experienced before. She stumbled in
the sheer strength of the power in the building. It came at
her, relentlessly, through the floor. She was dizzy.

Stitch appeared frozen. Jay followed the man's gaze as he
looked up into the higher levels. There were Readers there,
concealed. Jay felt their presence. The man stepped in front
of Stitch and turned to the control panel. He spoke, but Jay

couldn't hear what he said. She scuffed along the floor, edging closer. The energy from the floor and something coming from this man slowed her progress. She was still twenty feet away when the door next to Stitch swung open, controlled from the panel in front of the man. Then he shoved Stitch into the room before pressing another button to close the door behind him, sealing her friend in the cell.

The man turned to Jay, and she saw his name – *Hinton* – not from him, but from the minds of the Readers above them. He channelled their power somehow, and there were too many of them for Jay to resist. She closed her eyes and tried to summon as much of the energy of the Given as she could. She held up a barrier to the Readers, but it was weak. Hinton moved slowly towards her, an unsettling half-smile on his face. He was confident, felt no threat from Jay. Jay was weak. She needed the trees, the water and the earth to realise her full strength.

'Jay Macfarlane,' Hinton said. He emanated darkness, but not power. 'I want to show you something.' He turned to the nearest door and opened its control panel. The door swung open and before she could retreat, he reached out and took hold of her top, pulling her towards him like she was a rag doll. He flung her onto the floor of the room. The door clunked closed behind her.

Jay picked herself up and looked around the room, frantically searching for a means of escape. *Stupid*, she thought to herself as it sunk in how easily they'd been caught.

Nothing but steel walls, floor, ceiling. She could see that the chair too was made of metal. Within a few seconds, the door opened and Hinton entered. She tried her power on him. She was angry. She pushed into his mind.

A spike of pain pierced her chest and forced its way into her head. Her vision faltered, and she flopped to the floor, clutching her temples. This man's power was nothing she recognised. The pain intensified. Her world went black.

She came back to consciousness sometime later, her head throbbing. The room was empty. She was nauseous, confused. She struggled to her feet, using the wall to steady herself. Once again, the door swung open and Hinton entered. Jay could barely focus on him, her vision swimming and her body pulsating with waves of pain.

'She's ready,' Hinton said. Another figure appeared and led Jay to the chair in the middle of the room. He fastened her hands to the arms of the chair and removed her shoes and socks. He strapped her ankles to the chair legs before he and Hinton left the room. The door clunked closed.

Jay thought of the Interland, and of Zadie. She pictured Sasha Colden, her grandmother and the beginning of the power of the Given. As the image of Sasha floated in front of her eyes, she rested her head back to look at the ceiling.

Then it began.

The light in the room faded. Shadow edged towards her. Her own inner colours seeped from her body, the wisps of colour like gas leaking into the room, taking away the essence of her power. She closed her eyes and her head spun – faster and faster until there was nothing.

OTIS SHOVED Davey into the side of the tunnel, the concrete rings wet from the water leaking through from the outside. He'd had enough of his random choices of direction whenever they reached a junction. He spoke like he knew which way Jay and Stitch had gone, like he was some kind of expert tracker. But each time Otis listened to him, they ended up further away from the centre of the prison.

'Look,' said Davey. Let's just continue on this branch and take the next opening to the surface. If we're far from the centre, then we just work our way in, right?'

Otis released Davey's top and pushed himself away with a huff. He stormed off down the tunnel.

Earlier, Davey had spotted Jay from the window of the first floor of the pub that had been their resting place for the night. He gathered Otis, and they tracked Jay and Stitch, figuring that they'd need some help in their mission to free Cassie. Now, with Davey's poor tracking skills, they were probably a good way behind, and likely wouldn't catch them up in time to be of any use. Otis was determined to show Jay that he was on their side, the side of the Given, and that he could be an asset to the cause.

'Here,' called Davey. Otis stopped and turned back. In his fit of anger, he'd walked straight underneath a narrow shaft to the surface.

He backtracked to where Davey stood and looked up. 'Let's do it,' he said.

As soon as they emerged from the tunnel into the open, Otis felt the power of the Readers. It was concentrated on a building south of their location. Davey seemed to register what Otis was thinking. He nodded at Otis and then stood, moving towards the source of the power. Davey broke into a run, his long strides taking him to the cover of the low-rise buildings in no time. Otis reached him seconds later, puffing.

Otis sensed Readers, although no noise came from the building. He also felt the presence of the Given. 'Jay is here,' he said. Davey made to move into the building, but Otis held him back. 'Wait. Her power is weak. Tell me what you sense?'

Davey thought for a moment. He closed his eyes. 'Jay

and Stitch are here. Cassie too. Not much power. They could be shielded.'

'Can you feel the darkness?'

Davey nodded. 'Readers, for sure.'

'We go in covert. You shield for both of us. Let me see if I can get a fix on them.'

They stalked up the corridor. Otis felt the increasing energy of the darkness as they approached the central core of the building, a circular atrium. They stopped short, hidden behind the wall. Otis brushed his shaggy fringe from his eyes and scanned the room. Davey shielded with all of his level-7 power.

'Stitch is in there,' Otis said, motioning towards one of the steel doors. 'And Jay is in that one. I don't sense Cassie.'

Davey pulled Otis back as a man appeared on the other side of the room, heading towards the room that Otis sensed was occupied by Jay. Three others followed close behind the man, like guards protecting their General. The leader opened the control panel next to the door and pushed a button. The door swung open, and the men peered inside.

'Keep shielding,' whispered Otis to Davey.

As they watched, the leader waved away the other men, who retreated down the corridor. Then the man entered the room.

'Let's go. We get Stitch on the way through, then we take him out and get out of here. Grab that fire extinguisher.'

Davey pulled the red extinguisher from its housing and immediately struggled with its weight, almost dropping it. Otis focused his energy on the door behind which he knew Stitch was locked. As they approached, there was a clunk and a click as the door swung open.

'How...what -?' Davey started.

Otis interrupted, 'Stitch!' he shouted as Stitch launched himself at Otis and Davey.

Stitch took a moment to realise that it was Otis and Davey. His attack turned into a greeting as the three turned towards Jay's cell. As they did so, the man they'd seen from across the room emerged from the room and closed the door behind him. He turned to them.

The look of surprise on the man's face lasted just a second before Davey shoved the fire extinguisher into his face, knocking him to the floor.

* * *

SHOUTING from outside the door drew Jay in and out of consciousness. She opened her eyes a crack. All was dark but for a glow of light around the door. Then it was gone. She tried to move her arms, but her fingers wouldn't work. She slipped into darkness.

The door flew open, the noise and sudden light bursting into the room. Jay opened her eyes, seeing nothing but the light of the doorway and shadows moving through it.

'Jay, can you hear me?' a familiar voice.

'We'll have to carry her.' Jay now recognised Stitch's voice – frantic, pained. 'Davey, you and Otis help Jay up, I'm going to find Cassie.'

Jay felt her hands and legs as they were freed, a stinging pain on the inside of her left wrist. Someone on each side of her helped her to stand.

Someone touched the side of her face. 'Shit,' said Stitch. 'She has the scar.'

* * *

THE BOY SUPPORTING HER, Otis, pulled her across the yard towards the storm-water shaft. In front of them, someone else was shouldering Cassie. Stitch led the way. Feeling was coming back to her legs, and she moved them to help Otis. Stitch was the first to reach the opening to the shaft, followed by Davey and Cassie. Stitch flung open the metal hatch.

'Cassie?' said Jay.

Cassie flung her arms around Jay's neck. 'I knew you'd come, you idiot.' Cassie touched Jay on the side of her face. 'You have a scar. They reduced you.'

Jay's heart sank. She felt no power within her. She looked for a similar scar on Cassie's face. 'And you?' asked Jay.

Cassie shook her head. 'No.'

'Move,' shouted Stitch, motioning towards the steps down to the tunnel. 'Talk later.'

Jay looked over her shoulder, back to the building. No sign of any movement. 'What happened to Hinton?'

Stitch followed Jay's eyes. 'Otis and Davey happened to him. Slugged him a good one. He raised the alarm though, so the Readers will be on their way here from all over the unit. Won't take them long to figure out where we've gone.'

Davey put a hand on Jay's arm. 'You next,' he said. Jay looked him in the eye but couldn't read him. Her powers were weak. She felt nothing.

Stitch was the last to enter the shaft. Halfway down, Readers pulled at the hatch. 'Go,' Stitch shouted, pointing at the southern opening. Otis and Davey led the way, with Cassie and Jay following. Stitch hit the base of the shaft and launched himself after Cassie and Jay. More sets of feet land in the puddles at the base of the shaft. One, two, then three people. Then more. Reader after Reader. Stitch was at her back, a hand on her arm to urge her on. Cassie was up ahead with Davey and Otis. Jay's body ached, her head still pounding and throbbing like it had been emptied by whatever happened in that metal room. 'We need to pick it up,' Stitch shouted. 'They're gaining.'

At the second intersection, the Readers took the wrong turn. When Jay and Stitch reached the opening in the river wall, Otis, Cassie and Davey were standing at the precipice, looking out over the river, but the tide had risen, concealing the shore and blocking their path back to the steps to the road. There would be no way they'd be able to swim upstream against the flow, no way of knowing how far the next set of steps would be.

Stitch looked at Jay, then turned back into the tunnel. 'We can't go that way. We won't make it through the currents in the Thames. Who knows how far we'd need to swim.'

The sound of footsteps echoed through the tunnels. Getting closer. As the Readers emerged around the corner and scrabbled to a stop just a few feet from them, Otis linked arms with Jay. Davey did the same with Stitch, and Cassie joined. They turned, and together, they jumped.

The moment she hit the surface, the chain of arms broke. The cold water froze Jay's body and mind. Darkness blinded her. For what felt like minutes, Jay turned and tumbled in the water before crashing through the surface, gasping for air. She went under once more but returned to the surface quickly to take another breath. She was numb. Fear was the only thing keeping her blood pumping. She kept her head above the surface and stopped fighting against the water, instead summoning the power, the tendons of energy to take her to safety. She got nothing. No whispers from the water, no supporting energy, nothing. She felt empty – abandoned.

Jay struggled to keep her nose above the water, the currents pulling and jostling her. She scraped her arm on the river wall as she twisted and turned in the water. Voices. Up ahead, shouting. Stitch's voice. She strained to see. Two figures up ahead, out of the water and leaning out towards her. Stitch and Cassie.

Cassie held on to a railing on the steps as Stitch leaned out over the water, his hand stretched out. 'Take my hand,' Stitch shouted above the noise of the swirling water. But Jay was moving fast. Cassie leaned further out and Stitch stretched as far as he could. Jay thrust her legs down and projected herself up, hand outstretched for Stitch. He grabbed her wrist and clamped his fingers around her hand as she did the same. She jolted, pulling Stitch so that he almost followed her into the river. Cassie held firm, and Stitch's grip was sure. She drifted towards the river wall as Stitch and Cassie pulled her in. She scrambled up onto the concrete steps, bashing both knees as she desperately pulled herself from the water and collapsed on the steps.

'No time to rest,' said Stitch. 'The Readers will be coming. We need to find Samir.'

'Where's Otis, and Davey?'

'Gone to get to their motorbikes. We'll catch up with them later. We need to go.' Stitch dragged Jay to her feet; Cassie took her other arm and helped her up the steps. Back on the road, the wind felt like ice forming on Jay's skin.

Stitch looked up and down the road, trying to get his bearings. He pointed across the street towards an alleyway. 'There,' he said. 'Let's get off the road.' He grabbed Jay's arm.

'I'm OK,' said Jay. 'You go. I'm right behind you.'

Cassie and Stitch ran across the road as Jay caught a breath. As she stepped off the kerb, a Land Rover turned the corner and bore down on her. 'Jay,' shouted Stitch, turning as if to come back for her. Jay froze. The Land Rover stopped directly in front of her, close enough that she could see the look in the eyes of the Readers in the front seats. They stared at her, as if daring her to run. Before they could open their doors, Jay turned and ran as fast as she could towards Stitch and the alleyway, pursued by the sound of feet hitting the tarmac. Jay and Stitch followed Cassie into the warren of alleyways, taking random turns at every intersection. Still the Readers followed Jay.

Stitch took the lead. 'This way.' They poured out of the end of an alleyway into a yard area with a row of garages. 'Here,' said Stitch, running towards the garage at the end where he'd left Samir with the car. They slammed into the wall of the garage, its doors open.

Empty.

The car had gone.

No sign of Samir.

'No,' shouted Stitch, doubling over, his face in his hands. Jay turned just as three men ran from the alleyway, looking in both directions. They spotted Jay. Just fifty feet between them. Jay could not run any further. If this was her fate, to be taken by the Readers, then so be it.

The Readers closed the distance between them like they were in no hurry. Stitch slumped to the floor.

A roar of an engine from the side street. Lights. A car screamed around the corner and slid to a halt next to them. The Readers froze for a moment, then ran. Samir screamed something in Arabic before Stitch opened the passenger door and jumped in. Cassie reached for the back door and flung herself across to the other side, leaving space for Jay. Like a rabbit in headlights, Jay froze, her feet stuck to the floor. She stumbled, banged her knee on the car as Samir pulled away. A Reader was on her, his hand on her arm.

Cassie's hands on Jay's other arm. Samir picked up speed, Stitch screaming into his face to put his foot down. Jay squeezed herself away from the Reader's grasp. She tried to summon her powers but got nothing. The Reader looked into her, then turned to look at Cassie before clutching the sides of his head, squirming in pain. Cassie and Stitch both stared down the Reader, digging into him, disabling him. He stumbled and fell as the car picked up speed. With Cassie's help, Jay threw herself into the back of the car and Samir swerved around the corner and onto the main road.

26

Hinton looked out over the tops of the prison buildings towards the hills in the south. The midday sun had burned through the morning clouds and he could feel the warmth on his skin. He dabbed his fingers on the back of his head where his hair was matted with dried blood. The two boys that attacked him had approached shielded. He felt humiliated but undefeated. The outcome would be the same. Jay had already been reduced, and without Jay, the Interland was unprotected.

He pulled back his left sleeve and itched his stub where it attached to the prosthetic. The wound was long healed, but sometimes he still felt his hand, his wrist, his phantom number. Cutting off his own arm at nineteen years old was a small price to pay. Hinton rejected the power, rejected the membership of a club he never asked to join.

The path of the Given, the path that his parents both took, was not for him. The energy of the Given had brought him physical pain no one understood. With the physical pain came a psychological deterioration, a depression that infected every cell of his body.

The day came when he couldn't stand it anymore. His pain and depression had already affected his family, split their lives in two. His mother left not long after his nineteenth birthday, and his father remained distraught for months after. That day, in his father's workshop, with the band saw his father used for the logs sawn from fallen branches, he cut the Given out of his body.

If his father had been another five minutes, he would have bled out on the workshop floor, and if he'd got there two minutes earlier, they said, his arm might have been saved.

The false limb was his reminder of the power he once held, and his connection to the Given. Over the weeks and months that followed his discharge from hospital, as he learned to use the prosthetic arm, a new power grew within him. It was nothing like the painful energy that had been the power of the Given. This new power was in harmony with his body, was something that completed him, and it was unique. With his extreme action in rejection of the power of the Given and all its energy of natural sources, came something else – a power that couldn't be detected by the Given, a power with an unknown source that even Hinton didn't understand. What he sensed was that his power came from deep within the earth. Not from the land, the sea, and all living things, like the Given, but from the core, the heavy metals, the ore. He needed no Interland to exercise power.

'Sir?' A Reader approached Hinton on the roof. 'We lost them in the City. They split up into two groups and got away in vehicles.'

Hinton continued to inspect his prosthetic arm. 'When did you transform? Become a Reader?'

The Reader stumbled over his words. 'Me... Sir? I... Six years ago now, Sir.'

'And what level Given were you before you transformed?'

'Level three. Now a level six Reader.'

'There's a level of commitment that comes with the honour of being a Reader, you know that?' The Reader nodded. 'And with that commitment, from all of us, we control the Given, yes?'

'Yes, Sir.'

'So whose lack of commitment caused the failure today? Whose commitment so failed that we allowed two outsiders to walk through open doors to get to our most valuable prisoners and walk out unopposed?'

'I don't think it was...'

'You know,' the man interrupted. 'That I can reduce any Reader at the touch of a button?' The Reader nodded and lowered his gaze. Hinton pulled his sleeve down to cover his false limb. 'Anyway. The 8C has been reduced, so the Interland is unprotected. We can progress.'

'The Readers are ready to move out on your instruction, Sir.'

'We leave in the morning,' he said, thinking about his wife, and his little girl, Megan. 'We bring all Readers above level six.'

'That could be thirty Readers. Do we need that many?'

'We rendezvous at the Gateway, make sure everyone has the co-ordinates.' The Reader hesitated as if wanting to say something more. Hinton looked at him. 'What?'

'What do we expect to find when we get there?'

'Not your concern. Just get everyone ready. Without an 8C at the gates, the Interland is mine for the taking.'

'But sir. What about Zadie Lawrence?'

Hinton nodded. 'She'll see the higher purpose, particularly when she realises how powerful she can be as a Reader.' Hinton clapped the Reader before him on the back. 'Don't worry! I'm sure you'll get used to answering to her command.'

* * *

IN THE BACK of the car, Jay drifted in and out of sleep as Samir drove them to the agreed meeting place with Otis and Davey, where they could rest and take stock.

Jay's conscious moments were filled with anxiety and sadness. She felt no power. Her mind was deathly silent. No whispers, no feelings. She turned over her hand to look at her wrist. Her skin from the base of her hand almost to her elbow was a fiery, angry red. Through the red wounding, like a burn, there was no decipherable number. The 8C was no longer there, or at least no longer visible.

Cassie leaned over to Jay in the back seat and examined Jay's wrist. 'Looks sore,' she said.

Jay nodded. 'You?' she asked.

Cassie shook her head and revealed her own wrist, which showed her level seven marking, untouched by her experience in the sink-room. 'They wanted my power to remain with me so that I'd attract you. It was a trap. Right from the start, they took me and...' Cassie trailed off, her voice choked. 'They took me and killed Reuben. But what they wanted was you. It's my fault, we should have known...'

Jay silenced Cassie with a hand on her arm. Stitch leaned into the back from the passenger seat. 'We're meeting at Highdown. Samir knows a route up the west slope that we can take the car closer to the summit. Not sure you've got much walking in you, Jay?'

Jay shook her head.

Cassie said, 'I thought that route was impassable.'

'Me too,' said Stitch.

'Not if you know it like I do,' said Samir from the driver's seat. 'You kids don't know everything, you know. Wisdom comes with age.'

Jay rested her head on Cassie's shoulder. She had only enough energy to open her eyes and communicate for a few minutes before needing to rest again. She would be no use to them now, to the Given, or to the Interland. One more encounter with a Reader would kill her.

PART IV

27

As soon as Stitch and Cassie set Jay on the ground at the summit of Highdown, she curled up and drifted back to sleep. Stitch had defeat in his eyes. He placed a jumper under Jay's head as a pillow. 'Do you have something we can cover her with?' Cassie rummaged in her bag and dragged one of her own jumpers over Jay.

Stitch turned away. 'I'll get wood,' he said. Samir followed him into the trees.

Cassie put a hand on Jay's head, lightly touching the scar on her face. It looked identical to the wound that killed Reuben. Cassie left Jay to sleep and approached Otis and Davey, deep in discussion. 'What do you think?' asked Otis.

'About what?' replied Cassie.

'I say we get moving. Let's get to the Interland before these Readers can regroup and get there themselves. If we wait, the Interland will be taken.'

Cassie admired his spirit. Otis was small, but he was full of energy and fight. Davey didn't look so sure, looking past Cassie to where Stitch and Samir had melted into the trees. 'You might be right,' Cassie said. 'But without Jay...' She looked back at where Jay lay motionless. 'What chance do we have against the Readers?'

'Exactly,' said Davey.

Otis shifted on his feet. 'That's all I'd expect from you,' he said to Davey. 'There's more to this than survival. What are *you* going to do? Hide out and hope it all blows over?'

'Like you've been doing, you mean?' Davey hit back. 'Living up here in the hills, away from reality.'

'I had no choice. I had no idea about the Interland until I met Jay and Stitch.'

'Hey,' Cassie said, raising a hand between Otis and Davey. She felt conflicted. She owed the Interland nothing. Yet...

'I'm with Otis,' Cassie said. 'We have to do something. For the sake of the rest of the Given still back at the Interland. But it's Jay we need to get into the Interland. It needs the 8C and the C to protect it from the Readers.' Cassie thought of Jay's little brother, Sammy. She cared for him deeply, like she cared for Reuben. And now Reuben was dead. She couldn't face another loss.

Stitch and Samir arrived back at the camp, arms laden with firewood. Cassie helped Samir construct a fire while Stitch went to Jay. Samir broke up the smaller sticks for kindling, carefully placing the wood, and re-placing anything that Cassie contributed. She laughed and sat back, allowing Samir to finish the arrangement. 'Stitch,' Cassie called. 'Lighter?' Stitch threw over his lighter and Cassie handed it to Samir. 'Do the honours,' she smiled.

Samir lit the fire and Cassie sat back. She looked over at Stitch and back to Samir, trying to see the family resemblance. 'What?' said Samir.

Cassie shook her head. 'You two talking again. It's good.'

'Yes,' said Samir. 'I did a lot of thinking over the months

Stitch was away from me. His mother left us some years ago, and I was suddenly alone.'

'You and Stitch both,' said Cassie.

Samir looked Cassie in the eye, his dark irises reflecting the flicker of the flame from the fire. 'I know that now,' he said. 'My son and I were together, but alone. His letter made it very clear, but then he was gone. Disappeared into thin air with you and Jay. Like they say, you don't know the value of something until it is gone.'

'True enough,' said Cassie, looking around at the trees stretching up above the ledge on the summit of Highdown, where Reuben had fallen. She'd once taken freedom for granted. Not now, not when it was so fragile. It seemed inevitable that it would soon slip away from them for good.

'Then Allah brought him back to me,' he smiled. 'And this time I'll not let him go. This time we will stick together.' He turned back to the fire to load more sticks.

Cassie looked over at Stitch. He had his hand on Jay's head and his eyes closed as if he were trying to read her. 'Hey? What's up?'

Stitch opened his eyes and turned to Cassie. He pulled his hand away from Jay, frustrated. 'Nothing,' he said.

'Tell me,' said Cassie.

Stitch stepped over to sit with Cassie by the fire. 'You know I've been trying to develop the other side of my powers, the stuff that's not connected with Jay?' Cassie shook her head, a quizzical look on her face. Stitch rarely confided in her. There had always been an invisible barrier between them that prevented a deeper connection. 'Like with Sammy,' Stitch continued. 'That day we arrived at the Interland and Sammy was injured, you know?'

Cassie nodded. 'I remember.'

'I helped him.'

Cassie held Stitch's eye for a moment. 'You're talking about *healing*?'

Stitch nodded. 'Nothing miraculous, like mending bones or anything like that, but I'm pretty sure my focus dispersed the infection in him. I felt it.'

'What about Jay?' said Cassie, suspending her disbelief for a moment.

Stitch shook his head. 'Not getting anything. With Sammy, I had the time. I sat with him for hours in that place. We connected properly.' He lifted his sleeve for a moment, inspecting the black letter "C". 'I thought with my natural connection to Jay, I might be able to tune into her physiology like I did with Sammy.'

'Nothing?'

'I need her to fight. Why won't she fight?' said Stitch.

'She *is* fighting, she fought for me. She's the reason I got out of that place,' Cassie said.

Stitch said, 'That was more down to those two,' he nodded towards Otis and Davey. 'What I mean is why won't she fight for the power? She's been more scared of the source with every week that passed in there. It's like she won't trust herself to connect.'

Cassie looked at Jay, breathing steadily, her eyes closed. 'She's been through a lot. The fight against the Readers last time took a lot out of her. I'm not sure she ever really recovered.'

'Have you seen her wrist?' said Stitch. 'Her marking isn't there. Just a messy red mark, like a wound from a burn. She's been properly reduced.'

'Then we're screwed,' said Cassie. She nodded towards Otis and Davey. 'Otis is all up for storming over to the Interland, putting up a fight. I think Davey would rather curl up and hide up here. Without Jay's power... I don't know.'

'All we need to do is get her there, to the Interland and the source.'

'But what do you think she is afraid of?' said Cassie.

Stitch jumped to his feet. 'I've got an idea.' He called over Davey and Otis.

28

'In theory,' said Stitch. 'Jay can rebuild her power.'

'How?' said Cassie.

'If the folklore holds true, then the power can be rebuilt through the hill forts. I think that's what Zadie Lawrence did after she was reduced. After the hill forts, a return to the power of the Interland might be enough.' He paused, and the others remained silent. 'From what I read in the notebooks back at the Interland, if I'm interpreting it right, if Jay connects with all three hill forts, she'll be ready, like *primed*, to re-establish her powers at the Interland. Enough to repel the Readers.'

Davey huffed. 'You mean the Interland where the Readers are heading, with the source of power they're planning to destroy? The one Zadie Lawrence is opening up for the Readers? That's a fantastic idea, Stitch.' Davey stood and paced.

'And,' said Otis, 'how is she supposed to connect to the hill forts when she can barely open her eyes?'

Cassie groaned, scratching her head in frustration. 'By the time we get to the Interland, the Readers will already be there, and the source might already be gone. Which means that all this would be for nothing. None of us will have power.'

'Exactly,' said Davey. 'So what's the sense in going anywhere near that place. It would be suicide. We should move as quickly as we can in the opposite direction to the Interland. We need to hole up somewhere they'll not find us.'

Otis shook his head and kicked out at a stick by the fire. 'I've been holing up for long enough. I can't do it anymore, not after what we saw down there at the prison.'

'I'm with Otis,' said Stitch. 'We have to try before every Given ends up in a place like that. If we run, that's the end of the Given...'

'It's the end *anyway*,' said Davey.

'What would Jay do?' said Stitch, silencing the bickering.

Cassie thought about it for a moment. She wasn't convinced that Jay would run towards the Interland right now. She'd be more cautious than that. She'd be thinking of how to keep all of her friends and family safe. The only way they'd all survive this would be to get as far from the Readers as possible. But then there was Sammy. And Jay's dad, Ben. And the rest of the Given trapped at the Interland, held by Zadie Lawrence, if they were still alive.

'She'd go,' said Cassie. 'To the Interland. She'd do whatever she could to free the rest of the Given, by protecting the source. If there was even a chance of a future with at least a sliver of freedom, then she'd try.'

Stitch nodded. Samir nodded too in agreement. Davey sighed and sat back down. 'She would,' he said. 'The idiot. She would.'

* * *

THEY SHARED what food they had left and allowed Jay to sleep. After some time, Jay woke of her own accord and sleepily shuffled over to sit by the fire, pulling her jacket tight around her shoulders.

'Hey,' said Stitch as Jay squeezed to sit between him and Cassie.

Jay rubbed her eyes. 'How long have I been out?'

'Three days,' said Cassie with a smile.

Jay laughed, and Samir handed her a hunk of bread and a bottle of water. 'I feel better,' she said, taking a deep breath and looking up into the trees.

'Recharging?' said Stitch. He reached for Jay's hand and she allowed him to turn it over to have a look at her wrist. The redness had eased, and there was a smudge of a marking, a far cry from a distinguishable number, but something at least. 'It looks better,' said Stitch, looking to Cassie for confirmation.

Cassie nodded. 'You might be right.'

Jay looked between her two friends. 'Right about what?'

Cassie explained Stitch's plan for Jay to connect with each of the three hill forts before heading to the Interland and the source to complete her recharge, the re-establishment of her power.

'Connect? How?' asked Jay.

'Think about it,' Stitch said, an angry edge to his voice.

Jay startled at Stitch's tone. 'What's wrong?'

'This is serious. You need to look at yourself...'

'Stitch, ease up,' said Cassie.

'Ease up? No. I won't ease up. This is it, Jay. You need to decide where you are in this fight. Because if you don't wake up and see what's happening, then that's it for all of us. All the Given.'

'I...' Jay stammered. 'I don't know what you're asking me.

Tell me what I'm supposed to do and I'll do it. You saw the control that man had over us, all of us.'

Stitch held Jay's hands in his, pulling her around to face him. He spoke slowly. 'You need to dig deep,' he said. 'You *know* that you have a much deeper connection with the power. Your grandmother had it. You had it when you fought off Marcus. With me, your connection,' he squeezed her hands, 'you have the tools to control the energy. You can channel the source.'

'I can't,' Jay said.

'Are you scared to let it in? Scared of being unable to control it?'

'I can't untangle it,' Jay said, pulling her hands away. 'You've seen me. Every time we've tried to read the power down there it's knocked me down, and it's taken me days to recover.'

Stitch sighed, looking into the fire. 'It might be enough just to be there, in the Interland. That might be enough to keep the Readers out.'

'But, what-'

'We *have* to try, Jay.' Stitch's tone was firm. 'There is no other choice.'

Jay slumped, looking around at her friends. Cassie forced a smile. Otis nodded and Davey averted his eyes. Samir held Jay's eye for a moment, giving a gentle nod of encouragement.

'What's the plan then, Stitch?' She put a hand on his.

'I think you have to go there. To Cissbury and Chancton-bury,' said Stitch.

'Do we have time?' asked Cassie. 'We need to get to the Interland before the Readers get there. If they reach the source, and Zadie has opened the way, then there will be no power to replenish.'

'Exactly,' said Davey from the other side of the fire. 'It's too late.'

'Shut up, Davey,' said Otis, standing and approaching Jay. He knelt beside her. 'Look,' he said. 'We realise that this is a long shot. But, if we stand any chance at all, then it will be with your power, and your connection with Stitch here. And of course, our help.'

'I can't believe Zadie is helping them,' said Jay. 'Traitor.'

She stared into the fire and Cassie followed her gaze, watching the flames dance as if spinning the roulette wheel on their future.

Jay took a deep breath. 'OK. Let's do it.'

Otis cleared his throat. 'Great. I have an idea.' The others looked to him to continue. 'How about Jay do the tour of the hill forts and the rest of us head to the gateway place that Stitch was talking about, outside the Interland. We can pave the way, do a bit of recon, so that when Jay catches up, we're ready to go.'

'How will we get into the gateway, to the caverns?' asked Davey.

Cassie looked at Stitch. 'We can't hike through the Wilds again?'

'There must be a better way,' said Stitch.

Jay said, 'You can take the River Arun route. Stitch? It will be quicker, not so far to walk?'

'We don't know that route,' said Stitch.

'I do. From my dad's stories. I can give you directions to the Black Rabbit pub, then you follow the river.'

'What about you?' said Stitch. 'Shouldn't we stick together?'

'Like Otis said. I'll catch you up. I'll meet you in the main cavern. Don't go into the Interland before I get there.'

'I don't like the idea of leaving you on your own. I can help you.'

'You take the car. I'll use Davey's bike?' She looked at Davey and he nodded his agreement.

'I'll go with you,' said Cassie. 'You can ride on the back. There's no way I'm letting you ride Davey's motorbike. I saw how you handled that Vespa.'

'Stitch?' Jay said, as if asking permission.

He looked at Cassie, then back to Jay. 'Do it quickly,' he said. 'Head straight to Chanctonbury, then Cissbury. Then back to the Interland, right?'

Jay nodded. Cassie looked serious. 'Let's do it.'

29

Marcus turned the squirrel on the fire. He had grown thin over the past months, the food available in the surrounding woods insufficient to sustain his bulky frame. He would soon have to venture into a nearby town or farm if he were to survive.

He looked again at his wrist, an action he'd repeated more frequently in recent days as his sense of power strengthened. Since Cissbury. The energy of the land seeped into him as one of the Given, an ex-Reader – a Reader reduced to what he once was in the beginning. His marking was becoming more clear at every inspection, now undoubtedly a level six, a formidable power, though not his previous level eight as a Reader. Despite his weakened body, he felt the strongest he had since the conflict with Jay.

With his recuperation, Marcus felt changes in the air, something different in the movement of the trees in the wind, the clouds in the sky and even the way the rain scattered across the woodland floor. Since the Given had been forced to hide, no one was free outside of the Interland, except those like him acting the charade of freedom in a society led by Readers against the Given. In all this, Marcus had no identity. Worse than the Given in hiding, he was a Reader in his soul, with reduced power and diminished loyalty to the State. He was nothing. A man in limbo.

He finished his food. The fire burned down to embers, lulling Marcus into a sleepy daze. He cast his eyes up towards the other hill forts at Highdown and Chanctonbury. Highdown was dark. A light flickered at Chanctonbury at its highest point. Periodically, the light vanished, then reappeared as if intermittently obscured by someone, or something in the wind. As he watched, he felt something familiar, something he'd not felt in a while, a signature in the energy he felt coming over the Downs. He closed his eyes and listened. It was Jay.

There was someone else with her, someone with power. He wondered if it was Jay's brother, Sammy, the boy with Marcus's blood. The son he'd never known.

Jay was close, but her power was not as he remembered. She was weak. He felt an unfamiliar tingle of opportunity in his bones at the thought of Jay at less than full strength. Jay Macfarlane, the fabled level "8C", was vulnerable. The desire to settle the score between the most powerful of the Given and the most powerful Reader was strong. She was as vulnerable as she'd ever been since coming of age, and she was coming to Cissbury.

30

T he last steps to the summit of Chanctonbury, the second of the three hill forts, sapped Jay's strength. Her vision blurred; she longed to lie down. She and Cassie, both gasping for breath, entered the ring of trees. A group of teenagers drank cans of beer around a fire. Jay entered the inner circle and sat down on a log at the edge of the group. She was barely noticed. As soon as she sat, she felt an explosion of energy from the hill, the trees and from the sea on the horizon. It almost knocked her from her seat. Cassie stood next to her, eyeing the party-goers with suspicion, like a bodyguard. Jay looked up at Cassie.

'What?' said Cassie.

'Did you feel any of that?'

'A little...' Cassie said.

Jay stood. 'It was immense. Like a shot of adrenaline in the arm, like diving from a thousand feet into an ice-cold pool.'

'Nice,' said Cassie.

Jay spread her arms wide and took a deep breath. 'Let's

go!' She took Cassie by the arm and marched her back towards the bike.

* * *

BY THE TIME Cassie pulled the bike to a stop at Cissbury Ring, the energy had settled into Jay. She felt reinforced. They pulled off their crash helmets, and Cassie took a moment to look Jay in the eye by the light of the half-moon. 'Someone slip you something back on Chanctonbury?' she said.

'The energy took me by surprise.' Jay nodded to the summit of Cissbury. 'Let's go get more.'

A few hundred metres up the steep track, Jay experienced a different wave of energy, dark and foreboding. 'Cassie,' she called. 'Something's wrong. This could be a trap.'

'How? No one knows we're here. Even the Readers wouldn't be able to track us that quickly. We'll go carefully, approach from the north slope, not the main pathway, OK?'

They continued to the top and skirted around the north slope before pressing on towards the ring of trees. Cassie stepped over the final ledge but Jay stopped in her tracks, looking towards the east where beside makeshift camp and a smouldering fire, a man in dirty black clothes stood facing her. Jay knew immediately who it was, and her legs buckled. Marcus.

A scream came from over the hill, a piercing, determined shriek of fear just before Cassie flung herself over the ridge and into Marcus. They tumbled and Marcus landed heavily. Jay watched, still trying to catch her breath as Cassie took a fighting stance. Marcus struggled to his feet and

Cassie kicked out at him, landing several blows before he stepped away from her to summon his power.

His *power*. Jay thought to herself. What power could he have? He would have been reduced by their encounter. Cassie moved to kick out at him again, but he blocked and influenced her so that she slipped and fell back onto the woodland floor. She seemed to knock her head on something – a rock, or a tree root. She remained still as Marcus leaned down and checked on her before turning to Jay.

He walked slowly towards her. Jay's feet were rooted to the floor. She couldn't help but feel afraid in his presence. Her legs trembled as Marcus came close. His features were as she remembered – a little more gaunt, his body stringy and the bones in his face sharper. He stopped a few feet from her, and Jay could sense his weakened state. But she was weakened, too. She looked to the summit of the hill. Perhaps if she could reach the inner circle of trees, she'd stand a chance. She looked past Marcus to where Cassie lay motionless.

'She's OK,' Marcus said, his voice gravelly like he hadn't used it in a while. He cleared his throat. 'She knocked her head, she'll come around.' His face caught the light of the moon and his eyes revealed a new vulnerability. He raised his arm in front of him and pulled back his sleeve, showing Jay the black number six on his wrist. 'Thanks to you,' he said. 'No longer a level eight. No longer a Reader.'

Jay's mind raced.

'I suppose I ought to thank you,' Marcus said.

Cassie stirred in the background, pulling herself up to her knees and looking over to where Jay and Marcus faced each other under the canopy of the outer ring of trees. She jumped to her feet and started towards them.

Jay put up her hand. 'Wait, Cassie,' she said. 'Say that again,' she said to Marcus.

'I said I ought to thank you, for setting me back to neutral in the cavern that day. At the Interland. What you did,' he raised his hand to the two parallel scars on his face, 'brought me here. I've had some time to rebuild my strength, and my mind.'

Cassie gestured behind Marcus's back that she could take him out, now, from behind. Jay shook her head, her eyes back on Marcus. 'And what about your loyalties? Have they reset, too?' asked Jay.

Marcus gave a half smile and nodded up to the summit. 'Judging by your scar someone has attempted to reset you, too. Shall we head up, so you can soak up some energy?'

31

J ay placed a hand gently on Cassie's arm to reassure her that walking beside Marcus was safe. Jay's sense of Marcus told her he was a different man to the one she'd faced at the Interland. He was strong, for sure, but the source of his power, and motivation, had shifted.

Marcus sat on a log beside the remains of a fire in the middle of a circle of trees. Jay and Cassie sat opposite him and Jay immediately felt the energy seeping into her body – not like the hit of power she received at Chanctonbury, this time more of a steady, trickling recharge.

Cassie wasn't prepared to make amends so quickly with the man who'd recently hunted and attacked them all. 'This is the man that nearly killed Sammy. If it weren't for Stitch, your brother would be dead.'

'That was a different...'

'She's right,' Marcus interrupted Jay's defence. 'I was more than just one of the Readers. I led them. And I meant to do you harm.'

'We can't trust him...' Cassie said, standing.

'But I'm not that man anymore. However, the man who created the transformation process, he's still hard at work. His goals haven't changed.'

'Hinton?' asked Jay. Cassie returned to her seat next to Jay.

Marcus's head snapped up. 'You've met him?'

'That's one way of putting it,' Cassie said.

Marcus nodded. 'That explains your weakened state. He used to be one of the Given.'

'But he has no power,' said Jay.

'His power is different. He rejected the power of the Given and became something darker even than the Readers. He will be the end of the Given. There's nothing anyone can do about that. He will destroy the source sooner or later.'

'Not if we stop him,' said Jay. She scrutinised Marcus, trying to read him. He presented no shield and she could see he truly believed that Hinton and the Readers would destroy the source, and that the power of the Given, including Marcus's own power, would be neutralised.

He smiled a humourless smile. 'You don't look like you've been doing so well in that battle so far? You can't beat him on your own. Where's the boy? Stitch?'

'Heading back to the Interland,' said Jay.

'You'll need him.' Colours flowed from Marcus, not the familiar dark swirls that he emanated before, but streams of blue and orange that showed compassion. Jay looked to Cassie and could tell that she too could see them.

'You know there are other Interlands?' Marcus said.

Cassie met Jay's eye before they both turned back to Marcus. 'What do you mean?' asked Cassie. Jay thought back to the incident at the lake. What had happened with the man that sucked Jay and Stitch into the place with the dying islands, trees, and the multiple sources of energy no longer felt real.

'Our State, the authorities that run the Readers, is just one of eight worldwide superstates. Only those eight super-states have people with powers – a source, and some kind of *Interland*.'

'There are others?' Cassie breathed the words. Jay nodded at her friend. 'You knew?' Cassie blurted.

'And the Readers,' said Jay. 'They infect all of these states.'

Marcus lowered his gaze. 'I think so,' he said. 'The technology of the *transformation* started here, with Hinton, but other states have their own methods. There's a darkness that creeps into every pocket of light – a poisoned gas that is sucked into every vacuum. You can't stop it. It's inevitable.'

Cassie shook her head. 'I don't believe in fate,' she said.

Marcus laughed. 'It's not about *fate*,' he said, with a familiar venom. 'You can't reach a simple, stable balance in a world like this.' He gestured around himself. 'We have an innate sense of personal survival – a drive that comes before all else – which means we fight until the other side is neutralised. There's no other way.'

Jay recalled the withered islands that she and Stitch had been shown, where the darkness had enveloped their energy, squeezed their life away. 'If the Given are reduced, the Readers will command the ultimate power,' Jay said.

'Yes, and with the dominance of the Readers comes a more powerful darkness. A critical mass brings a flashover of power. A darker place than even I can imagine or understand.'

Cassie shifted in her seat. 'So this regime spreads like a virus, across all eight States?'

'And beyond,' said Marcus.

Cassie stood again. 'We've done enough sitting around talking, let's go.' She pulled at Jay's arm.

Jay resisted. 'Marcus,' she said. 'Show us that your allegiance has shifted. Prove yourself by coming with us.'

Cassie looked at Jay, incredulous.

Marcus shook his head. 'This is not my fight.'

'It's yours as much as it is ours,' said Jay. 'If the source is destroyed it takes your power too.'

Marcus raised his hand to touch the scars on the side of his face. 'I'm done. You're on your own. It would be a suicide mission for me. I can't take another transformation.' He shook his head. 'No, I'll live out my days here. The end will come whether I chase it or not.'

'There are others,' Jay said. 'Others with power that are hiding out across the country. Not all the Given have been taken in for rehabilitation.' Marcus looked up at Jay but said nothing. He stood and Jay stood with him. 'You are the Given now, Marcus. Show it. Connect with the rest of the Given on the outside.'

'Don't you remember?' Marcus said.

Jay gave him a quizzical look.

'How you did this?' He pointed to the scar on his face. 'If you want to fight this battle, you have to use your advantage. It's all you've got.'

'Hinton is different,' Jay said.

'Then *you* need to be different...'

'Jay,' urged Cassie, tugging at her arm. 'We need to go.'

'Help us,' said Jay. 'Link to the others on the outside. Bring them. Join us?'

'I don't have the reach, and even if I did...'

'Figure it out...' Jay said.

'Jay!' Cassie insisted.

When Jay turned back to Marcus, he had slipped away into the trees. She could take off after him, hunt him down and try to persuade him, or she could get back to the others before it was too late. She followed Cassie down the hill, back to the bike.

32

S amir sulked in the passenger seat. He'd wanted to drive, but Stitch insisted he rest. He hadn't stopped talking since they left Highdown, first complaining about Stitch's driving, then asking relentless questions about the Interland and the route they needed to take.

'Rest, Dad, please. We have a long walk once we get parked up.'

'How far is the walk? Will we be OK in this footwear? We should have come prepared. I have some walking boots at the house. Where are the walking shoes I bought you?'

Stitch ignored his dad. In the backseat, Otis and Davey spoke quietly, and Stitch couldn't catch what they were saying. They laughed, and Davey turned to look out his side window, a smile lingering on his face. A connection growing between them. Stitch thought of Jay, sensed she was OK, was growing in strength, but he felt disconnected without her. He felt alone.

'I'm not going on any river. If you think I'm getting on a raft made of logs then you...'

'Dad, please,' Stitch sighed. 'You want me to drop you home?'

Samir let out a resigned sigh. 'What will you do without me, eh? How will you navigate through the Downs?' Stitch smiled at his dad. 'So tell me about these stories that Jay's dad used to tell you. I don't know why you needed someone else to tell you stories, you never wanted to listen to my stories when you were little.'

'I did...' Stitch started, then thought better of it. 'He told us about a route to the Interland. It was something he'd got from a Runner back before the protest and the crackdown. Then he made it his own, you know, exaggerated it, embellished it with his own imagination, but the basic facts are there.'

Stitch looked in his mirror to see Davey and Otis leaning forward to hear Stitch's explanation. 'Back before the darkness...' Stitch used his exaggerated story-voice. 'When I was a young and handsome adventurer...' Samir laughed but motioned for Stitch to continue. Stitch told of the route to the Interland, much as Ben had told it. 'When we get to the river, we need to make a raft, and float through to the gateway.'

'Can we swim through?' said Otis. Out of the corner of his eye, Stitch saw Samir raise his eyebrows at the suggestion.

'Maybe,' said Stitch. 'But if we can float downstream, it might be easier.'

'Then what?' said Davey from the back seat.

'We wait for the others,' said Stitch.

Otis said, 'Me and Davey can do some recon.'

'We need to stay out of sight,' said Davey. 'No point in going in until Jay gets there.'

'Just a bit of recon. See how the land lies,' said Otis.

Stitch pulled the car into the car park of the Black Rabbit, facing the still moving water of the river. Its surface was a swirl and tangle of currents.

Samir spoke up from the backseat. 'This pub's been closed for months. Economy is in free fall.'

A sense of inertia prevented Stitch from moving. If he could just stay in the car. Opening the door would be the first move along a path that would see the Readers test them more than they'd been seen before. And all while Jay struggled to regain her stripped power. If Jay could not tap into the source of her power, then Stitch would be no use to anyone. His power and influence was contingent on the strength of Jay's power. And even then, who knew what they'd be up against.

He looked around the car – his dad, Otis, Davey. 'Let's go,' he said, sighed, and opened the car door.

CASSIE OPENED up the throttle and she and Jay raced through the hills of the Downs on Davey's bike. Jay's crash helmet had no visor, so the wind battered her face every time she dared to peek out from behind her friend. Tears dried on her cheeks in the wind, her skin becoming cracked and sore.

'Slow down,' she shouted in Cassie's ear. Jay had avoided trying to read Cassie, for fear of failing. She knew that her power had replenished to a degree, the developing mark on her wrist was evidence of that, but it was far from complete. The flow of energy through the earth, the environment, felt restricted. It was as if the channels were blocked, clogged, and she'd not yet figured out how to free them.

She watched the blur of the trees go by. These hills had

become her home, literally, as the Interland was where she lived, and what she considered her spiritual base. She'd always felt connected to the environment in a way that was still only slowly becoming clearer to her. Since she was a small child, she'd spent time out on the roof of her childhood home, building and developing a connection, an understanding with the energy of the land. The sea was her friend, the hills, her adventure, her challenge.

33

The trek through the thicket alongside the Arun was easy passage, the banks dotted with reeds and wildflowers. When the river opened out into the floodplain the beauty of the scene gave Stitch pause. He recalled Ben's stories. Here, the river flowed to a standstill, spreading out across the fields as if flopping down to rest after an exhausting journey. At the outlet from the flood-plain, the Arun flowed west over a small weir and on towards a dark hill that reached high above its neighbours.

'That must be the hill,' said Stitch.

Davey and Samir slipped off their rucksacks to ease the load on their shoulders. Samir sat down and wiped his brow with a handkerchief. He looked up past Stitch towards the imposing hill in the distance. 'So that's the Interland?'

'Not really,' said Davey. 'The Interland itself is under-ground, deep below that hill.'

'But the hillside there,' said Stitch, 'is our way in. There's an opening that will take us into the gateway.'

Otis wandered off. His rucksack lay on the ground next to Stitch. A moment later he returned. 'No boats,' he said.

'Anything we can use as a raft?' said Stitch.

'Logs? Wood?' said Otis.

'Why can't we walk along the edge of the river?' said Samir.

'It'll take too long,' replied Stitch.

Samir huffed, 'You lot swim or float or whatever, I'll keep my feet on solid ground.'

Stitch rolled his eyes. He nodded for Otis to follow him into the trees. They returned with a single log. Davey laughed. 'Is that it?' he said.

'Come on,' said Stitch. 'There's more.'

It took them an hour to gather materials and lash together a makeshift raft using straps from their backpacks. The four of them stood over the creation, studying it. Davey's frown deepened. 'Really?' he said.

They dragged the raft into the water and it dipped under before bobbing reluctantly to the surface. 'There's no chance that will hold all of us,' said Davey.

Otis huffed at Davey's pessimism and took the lead by throwing his rucksack onto the raft. Stitch did the same and then grabbed Samir's bag and placed it next to his on the raft. Samir looked worried but said nothing. Davey sighed and threw his own bag on before Stitch and Otis climbed aboard. The raft wobbled and lowered in the water. Stitch held out a hand for his dad and helped him into position in the middle of the raft, surrounded by the rucksacks. Davey climbed on last and positioned himself at the back of the raft.

'How do we steer?' said Davey.

'Just push us into the flow,' said Otis.

Davey pushed at the river bank until the raft caught the undercurrent and drifted slowly downstream. With the weight of all four, and the bags, the surface of the raft was barely above the water. Stitch could already feel his trousers getting wet as the water seeped up through the logs. 'Don't move around,' said Otis as the raft bobbed and the front edge dipped below the water.

After a minute or two the raft picked up a little speed and moved out into the middle of the river, heading for the weir. 'Shit,' said Otis. 'We didn't plan on going over this thing.'

'It's fine,' said Stitch. 'Just a little speed bump.'

The front of the raft slipped over the weir and Otis's legs were immediately below the water. As he tried to right himself, he went in, splashing like a drowning boy as he grasped for the edge of the raft. Stitch reached for him, which made the raft tip precariously, sending Stitch over-board. The cold took his breath away for a moment and when his head finally broke the surface, he gasped for breath and grabbed for the raft. Samir shuffled close to the middle of the raft, hugging the bags into him as Davey struggled to remain upright at the back which had now dipped into the water with the imbalance of weight. Davey screamed as he slipped into the water and came up for air a few seconds later.

'Shit,' said Stitch. He tried to climb back on to the raft as it picked up speed in the narrowing section of the river. Each time he tried, the raft listed and threatened to tip Samir into the water.

'Leave it,' said Otis. 'Hold on and we can drift down like this.'

'It's freezing,' shouted Davey from the back.

Stitch held on and kicked his legs to direct the raft as well as to try to keep warm.

They drifted. As they approached the hillside, the cave Stitch had heard about so many times in Ben's stories came into view. It emanated a foreboding darkness, and a deafening noise as they breached the opening. Through the hill, all four looked around themselves in fear and wonder, the darkness hiding the details of the rock face. Stitch's fear turned to excitement and anticipation as the light of the pool, the gateway, grew in the distance. He kicked his legs. Finally, they slipped into the pool. The journey was over.

* * *

CASSIE TOOK control of the boat from the back, digging the oars deep into the water, and guiding them downstream on the unnamed river. Despite the explosion of undergrowth since they'd last been here, the connection to the unnamed river had been easy to find. As the boat slipped through the caves and rock tunnels, Jay felt a familiar sense of magic. She felt at home.

Cassie stopped rowing, allowing the boat to drift. Ahead of them, the tunnel opened out into a cavern. The space opened up, its ceiling hundreds of feet above their heads, light penetrating to cast shards over the water.

The energy of the cavern caught Jay's breath, silencing her. She choked, dragging air into her lungs. Her head fell back, opening her airway, and her breath flowed full and open as she stared into the roof. The light intensified; energy coalesced into shapes. White light pulsated in front of her eyes, blinding her to the stone walls. A shadow appeared in her periphery. 'Stitch?' she breathed. No response. The only sound was the thumping of her own blood pumping through her veins.

The light poured down on Jay from above like an endless waterfall, pounding her face and her body. The shadow passed once more and settled in front of her – a figure, featureless but familiar. Without words, the shadow of energy settled with Jay.

'I don't know how,' Jay said into the light, the response to a silent question about why she would not open to the energy, a question only she could hear.

Whispers came at Jay, clear and decipherable. 'You are closed. Resisting.'

Jay shook her head. 'No.'

'You are closed,' the whispers repeated, over and over.

Jay shook her head and put her hands to her ears. All around her, the light began to recede, revealing the surface of the water, the boat, the walls of the cavern. She looked over her shoulder, expecting to see Cassie. She was nowhere in sight. She looked back into the roof of the cave and the whispers came once more. 'You are closed,' came the message.

34

S ammy crawled through a gap little wider than his chest. He had to twist his shoulders and scrape them through before popping out the other side. The others remained at the drop where Toyah lay, unconscious. Sammy was conscious of the need to be quick. He'd left them just over fifteen minutes ago. Deep in the underground, he had never felt so lonely. He thought of Cassie and tried to channel her confidence and determination. Then he thought of Toyah, and how he'd led her into such danger with no certainty that there was anything at the end.

He stood straight for the first time in hours, the space finally big enough. He shone his torch left and right through the tunnel he'd landed in, then back up to the crevice he'd crawled through, incredulous that he got his body through such a small space. The sound of trickling water washed a sense of hope through his body. It echoed, as if flowing into an open space. A welcome relief from the deadened sound of the tight spaces he'd been in for what seemed like hours.

Pinto and Alfred had insisted Sammy press ahead. He was their only chance of finding a route out. He would find it, then he would head back to them and lead them out. Pinto had taken Sammy's hands. To help with the first few steps into the darkness, Pinto suggested they fly over the ledge and see around the first corner, just to be sure. Together, Sammy and Pinto had connected, left their bodies with Toyah and Alfred, and passed through the narrow opening and into the wider cavern. The view was enough to give Sammy the confidence he needed.

Sammy leaned down and picked up a lump of limestone. He used it to mark a line on the black wall at the location of the opening in the roof through which he'd emerged. He finished his artwork with an arrow pointing up, and a smiley face that was more a hope than a reflection of his feelings. He moved toward the welcoming sound of flowing water.

Just a few minutes passed before Sammy turned a corner and hit a dead end. 'No...' he breathed into the darkness, the light from his torch barely effective in the gloom. There was no longer a sound of running water. He retraced his steps, moving slowly this time, feeling his way through the black hole, his hand dragging along the rocks as if he were reading in braille.

'Here.' Sammy spoke to himself aloud, to convince himself he wasn't alone. He stopped. He shone his torch and moved to the edge of the tunnel where it opened into a wider section. At the far edge, at the floor, a sliver of light showed through a discontinuity in the rock. He could hear the distant sound of running water. A waft of fresh air blew over his face and he closed his eyes. He clambered over the edge of the opening in the rocks and slid sideways through the gap.

Just a few minutes of squeezing through narrow passageways and Sammy dropped into another open section, a cave with no obvious entry or exit but for the gap he'd crawled through and a wide hole in the floor into which water gushed. He shone his torch into the abyss and saw nothing but blackness. He could hear that the hole was full of water, from around ten feet down, although he could barely see its surface. He sat, exhausted. Hope, so tentatively grasped, seeped from him. He wasn't even sure he'd be able to climb back through those caves to the others if he had no good news for them. He rubbed his fists into his eyes, fighting tears, then caught a twinkle of light through a hole about halfway up the cave wall. Was he imagining it?

It took a moment before he could focus. He blinked away the stinging sensation and looked again. He gasped at the sight of the chalk cliffs around the turquoise water of the deep pool. He recognised it immediately as the gateway, the hole through which he, Jay, Cassie and Stitch had fallen all those months before. He was somewhere halfway up the cliff. Above the location where the River Rother discharged into the pool. He looked back into the cave and allowed his eyes a moment to adjust to the darkness. 'The Rother,' he said to himself aloud. 'This is the Rother.'

The pool at Sammy's feet was a deep well of water, only ten feet across but likely fifty feet deep. This was the head of pressure that Stitch had explained to them when they were back at the gateway. The pressure would build to a point that it became too much for the blockage, and then it would push itself out into the pool outside. All he needed to do was wait for it to blow.

* * *

IT TOOK Sammy less than half an hour to get back to the others. His sense of relief was overwhelming as he climbed the final few feet to the ledge and saw that Toyah was awake. She lay on the rocks with her head on Pinto's lap, but her eyes were open and she strained to give Sammy a smile as he emerged from the deep. 'Toyah,' he said, placing his hand gently on her shoulder as if he might break her.

'Find us a way out?' she asked.

'Of course,' said Sammy.

'Really?' said Pinto. Toyah sat up, then leaned back onto the rock as if dizzy.

'Steady,' said Alfred. 'You've had a nasty knock. I'm not sure you should move anywhere. How far is it, Sammy?'

'Not far. She can't stay here. I'll help her through.' He looked at Toyah. 'If you think you can do it?'

'I can do it,' she said.

'And how are you?' Sammy asked Alfred.

He moved his foot in a tight circle, wincing. 'It's not broken, but it hurts like hell.'

'I'll help you,' said Pinto.

Alfred smiled and put a hand on Pinto's head. 'You will, young man. I'm relying on you to get this old man out.'

TOYAH AND ALFRED rested at the top of the well that was full of the River Rother as Sammy explained the mechanism for the blowout. Pinto looked up at Sammy. 'You're kidding?'

Sammy shook his head, 'Trust me,' he said, trying to keep a positive tone to his voice. The level of the pool was almost at their feet, at the lip of the hole. Sammy thought for a moment that the water might rise through the rest of the cave before the pressure was enough to blow, but looking around the floor of the space, he could see that it was permeable. When the water flowed over the edge, the pressure would be at its highest. 'Get ready,' he said.

'What for?' said Alfred.

'When it blows, I'm not sure how long we will have to get ourselves down this well and out through the connection. Might just be a few minutes.'

'How do you know it will not be just a few seconds?' asked Pinto.

Sammy didn't answer.

A deep gurgling emanated from the depths of the pool. Sammy looked at Toyah, her face a picture of fear. Alfred too looked worried. The gurgling subsided and there was a movement in the ground beneath them. A rumbling. Then an almighty noise – rock, water, debris moving through the caves. The water in the pool bubbled for just a fraction of a second and then disappeared in an instant as it flushed through the hole and into the outside world. As it disappeared, light flooded the cave from below.

Pinto screamed with delight and even Alfred stretched to a smile. Sammy leaned over the hole and saw that there was a passable route to climb down. 'Let's move,' he said. But Toyah was already on her feet.

'I'll go first,' said Sammy. 'You follow. Go slowly. I'll guide you.'

At the bottom of the well, they entered a horizontal passage that led to the outside. Sammy could finally see the open air. An almost circular oasis of light at the end of the passage. Water flowed at their feet as the Rother passed freely down the well and along the tunnel to discharge into the pool. Behind them, in the rock passageway, Sammy could see that the surrounding ground mass, a mix of rock and clay soil, had already moved part way to re-block the passage of the Rother. It would be just a matter of minutes before the passage would be blocked once more and the well would fill again. 'Let's go,' he said. But Pinto was already running full speed towards the opening, to the outside, beyond the protection, and imprisonment, of the Interland.

35

It was dark by the time Stitch had the fire going in the main cavern, their clothes hanging on rocks to dry. Otis paced the cavern as if reading its history in the walls. He ran his hand along the uneven rock as he walked towards one of the openings, a connection to one of the multitude of interconnected limestone caves.

'Don't get lost through there,' said Stitch.

Otis turned and made his way back to the fire. 'We can dry off a bit and then see what we can find, eh Davey?' he said.

Davey nodded, but Stitch disagreed. 'We should wait for Jay. The Readers could be in there already.'

'No,' said Otis. 'If they were here, the source would be destroyed and there'd be no power. I can feel we still have power.' Otis felt invincible, aching to explore his power. He knew he had something different as a level five, the ability to affect solid objects, to move things, but had never used it with any conviction. 'We need to go in. It's too risky to wait. If Jay gets here after the Readers, then there will be no more of the Given to fight. We can at least find out what's going on, so that when she gets here, we can make a plan.'

'He's right,' said Davey, a reluctant smile in Otis's direction. 'As much as I'd rather snuggle up by this fire, we need to go in. We're here now. If we wait, like Otis says, it could be too late.'

Stitch sat next to Samir. 'If you two go, I'll stay with my dad, wait for Jay.'

'You go,' said Samir. 'I'll be OK.'

Davey shook his head. 'Stay with Samir. We don't need to be leaving people on their own right now, we stay in twos.'

Samir agreed. Stitch headed over to what remained of a set of shelves on the wall of the cave. He found a scrap of paper and took a pencil from his bag before sitting back down. 'I'll draw you a sketch of the layout up there,' he said to Otis.

THE LEVEL of the unnamed river was low enough that Otis and Davey could easily wade upstream to the connection. They might have missed the opening in the roof had Otis not sensed it. Otis helped Davey up so that he could pull himself through the hole and give a hand for Otis to follow.

They edged towards the inner caves of the Interland, stopping at the waterfall pouring from the roof, masking their way like a giant, shimmering curtain. Otis peered through a gap in the flow, and, seeing that there was no one on the other side, slipped through, wiped water from his eyes and backed up against the rocks out of sight. Tense, raised voices came from the main cavern. Davey leaned out from the rocks to see into the cavern, but Otis pulled him back.

Otis nodded towards a darkened alcove on the other side of the passageway that would make a better, more hidden vantage point.

Davey went first, Otis followed, hesitating at the sight of a woman sitting at the long dining table in the cavern, flanked by armed men in tense conversation.

Davey said, 'That's Zadie Lawrence in the middle.'

Otis took her in. She was not the giant of a woman that he had in his mind – the dominating presence and formidable power who led the infamous protest and commanded the respect and loyalty of the Given. This woman was small, unthreatening. But as Otis watched, she seemed to grow in stature. People stopped to ask her questions, and she gave directions with authority. Her control over those around her was impressive. They lowered their heads when she spoke, as if nervous of revealing their minds, and scared to appear to contradict.

'The two men beside her are Simon and Jared.'

Otis looked around the cavern. He could see a picture on the wall behind Zadie, hanging at an angle like it had been knocked. Davey nodded towards the far end of the cavern. 'Look.'

'What?'

'The opening in the roof. The whole of the upper part of the cavern has been blown away. It's opened up, and the passageway is blocked.'

It looked like there had been a landslide. A pile of rocks and stone rested along one side of the cavern. Daylight pierced the underground gloom where trees and branches slipped into the cavern. Water dripped through and a rope ladder, with wooden rungs, led from the cavern floor up into the trees beyond.

Otis motioned towards the pile of rocks that blocked the main passageway into the depths of the Interland. He saw a passageway off to the side. 'What's through there?' he said.

'That leads down to the source.'

Otis ached to see the source, touch it, feel its power. He looked back at Zadie and her companions. He put a finger to his lips to quieten Davey so that they could listen to them for a minute.

One of the men spoke. 'Use the source. Can't that tell you when they'll be here?'

Zadie shook her head. 'I don't need the source. I already know Hinton is on his way, with numbers.' Zadie lowered her head and Otis felt a wave of regret wash across the cave.

'There are Given trapped in there,' Otis said to Davey. 'What's she doing?'

'She doesn't know,' said Davey.

'Know what?'

'She doesn't know that the Readers intend to destroy the source. She thinks it's a peaceful union, but the Readers have other ideas. If they destroy the source, she loses her powers the same as the rest of the Given.'

'Then we can tell her,' said Otis, edging forward.

'Wait,' said Davey. Zadie had risen from her chair and was heading towards them.

'What is it?' said one of the other women.

Zadie stopped. 'If Jay and Stitch are alive, there's a risk that this all fails.'

'But she's been reduced. You know that?'

Zadie nodded. 'I know what they said. And I can feel that her power is not what it was. But she is strong. She has been underestimated before, and I won't do the same.'

'What about Davey?' said one of the men. Davey stiffened at Otis's side, holding his breath as he listened. 'Use the source to connect with him and find out what's going on.'

'He's no longer with us.'

'Dead?'

'No. He tried to mislead us. He said that Jay was dead. I can't trust him.'

'If she is reduced,' said the man, 'then she won't come here, she's no longer a concern.'

Zadie stepped towards the man and grabbed him by his shirt. 'Look at this.' She spat her words as she tilted her head to show the man her scar. 'I was reduced. Do I seem like I have no power to you?' The man shook his head. 'Power can be replenished. And if she comes here, and can get access to the source, then she could regain her power. Maybe not immediately, and maybe not back to what she had before, but we can't take the risk.'

Zadie looked to the entrance to the source, then back to her companions. 'How much explosive do we have left?'

'It's in the store. What are you thinking?' said Jared, a tall, spindly man with greasy black hair.

'We block off the access to the source. For good. Do it right.'

Davey and Otis looked at each other in horror. 'We can't let them destroy the route to the source,' said Otis. 'If these rocks come down they'll never be opened again.'

'What can we do?' said Davey. 'They're armed. And there's no way we can face up to Zadie's power.'

Otis needed to make use of his power, his unique nature of the level five. He closed his eyes and relaxed his muscles, connecting with his inner energy. The power came quickly. His proximity to the source was obvious in the way the energy flowed through to his arms, legs, his fingertips. He opened his eyes to see that Davey was staring at him.

'What are you doing?' said Davey. Otis revealed the number five on his wrist. 'I know,' said Davey, 'but what does that mean, what can you do?'

Otis smiled. 'Watch.' Three mugs and a pile of plates wobbled at the far end of the table and then slid sideways with a force that took them smashing into the wall of the cavern. Zadie and the others physically jumped and then recoiled from the disturbance.

Zadie stood and marched to where the plates lay smashed on the floor. She picked up a piece of broken crockery and stood, studying it. After a moment she looked up and around the cavern as if looking for someone. 'Shield,' said Otis as Zadie's energy felt its way through the cavern.

Otis began to shake from his feet through his body to his head. He'd never moved objects to this extent before. The reaction pulsed through his body. He felt wired. His face flushed, and he glowed. The trembling grew worse, and he throbbed with energy. Stones from the floor of the cave rose as Davey and Otis watched. They hovered in the air a few feet from the ground across the width of the tunnel. If Zadie or one of her men looked in their direction, they'd surely see. Davey shoved Otis, but it made no difference. Otis was no longer in control.

Zadie and the group split, three of them heading out towards the source and three, including Zadie, heading towards the passageway where Otis and Davey hid. Otis closed his eyes again, connecting with the energy.

'We need to go,' said Davey.

'Shh...' said Otis as he opened his eyes and felt the energy surround him. The stones dropped to the floor, and he turned his attention to the gun in the hand of the man who stood with Zadie. He moved it, twisting it out of the man's hands and dropping it to the floor.

'Careful,' said Zadie, glaring at the man. He leaned down to pick it up, confusion on his face. As he reached for the gun, Otis flung it across the floor of the cave and out of reach. Zadie looked after it, a glimmer of understanding in her face. 'We have a level five in our midst.'

'Otis,' Davey whispered. 'We can still make a run for it.'

Otis shook his head. 'It's time.' As he said these words, he stepped out into the open. Without guns, Zadie and her two colleagues stepped back as Otis stepped forward.

'Who are you?' asked Zadie, raising her arm to prevent her two colleagues from advancing on Otis.

'We're on your side,' said Otis. The other three returned to join Zadie's group. Two of them were armed. Jared raised his gun. Otis used his power to push it back down. Zadie watched, impressed.

'You're a level five,' she said. Otis nodded. 'How did you find this place?'

'We know what you're doing, and you're making a mistake.'

'How's that?'

'The Readers are coming here to destroy the source.'

'This is about integration. No more fighting,' said Zadie. Jared leaned in to whisper something that Otis didn't hear but sensed. Jared wanted to end the discussion and was planning to use his gun. Zadie held out a hand once more to calm her friend. 'Who are you with?'

'It's just me,' said Otis, but he could read that Zadie already suspected that he was there with Jay and Stitch, and she was nervous. 'If you let them in here, and they destroy the source, then that will be the end of the power for all the Given.'

'What do *you* suggest?' Zadie remained calm.

'If you allow Jay and Stitch back in here, they can ensure the protection of the Interland. With you, with your power, and Jay's connection, the Readers won't be able to enter. This can be the sanctuary it was meant to be.'

'Bit late for that.' Zadie motioned towards the gaping hole in the roof and the blocked passageways. 'There's no reason for the Readers to destroy the source. This is the root of all power. Without it, the Readers are nothing.'

Otis drew a breath. 'You don't know.'

'What?' said Zadie, frustration leaking into her tone.

'The Readers, Hinton, whatever he is, they don't draw their power from the source. Not anymore.'

Zadie laughed, a humourless smile on her face, a glimmer of uncertainty. 'Everything with power draws from the source.'

Otis shook his head. He sensed that Zadie had some level of belief in Otis's claim, but was burying it. She wasn't able to connect with the truth. Hinton had some level of control and influence over her.

'So what's your plan?' asked Zadie. Otis said nothing. 'And Jay? Where is she?'

'Why are you so scared of her?' asked Otis.

Zadie took a step towards him. 'I'm afraid of no one. You see all this,' she said. 'This was supposed to be mine. I am the one who rallied the support, led the way here when Sasha Colden passed. The Given were nothing when I took over this place. There was no one else out there taking the fight to the State. Then comes Jay with her marking, and Stitch. Who'd have known that there could be another like Colden?' Zadie lowered her gaze.

'She came to *join* you, not fight against you,' said Otis.

Zadie had anger in her eyes. 'Jay's not here. I'd be able to feel her. She's gone, hasn't she? That's why you're here, to talk me out of this?' Otis shook his head, but Zadie continued, stepping closer. Jared retrieved his gun from the side of the cavern, and Simon now also had his hand on his gun. The power flowing through from Zadie rose, and Otis felt his own energy under attack. Jared raised his gun and Otis pushed Jared's arm down. Simon pointed his own gun at Otis and could not deflect both of them.

'Do it,' said Zadie, her expression one of sheer determination, her teeth clenched.

As the sound of the shot rang out, Otis felt Davey pull him from behind into the alcove. He bashed his head against the rock with the force of Davey's shove. The distraction took Otis's power away from its target, releasing Zadie's gunmen. Otis heard three more shots but felt nothing.

Davey slid to the floor behind him, lifeless.

'No!' Otis screamed.

Zadie moved fast, staring at Davey on the floor, a quizzical look on her face. She knelt near, recognising him. 'Davey,' she whispered. She checked his pulse and looked up at Jared. She shook her head. Otis ran from the confinement of the alcove, towards the waterfall. His only thought was that if he could make it before Jared lifted his gun, then the water would conceal him and he stood a chance of escape.

A warning shot. Otis froze steps from the waterfall, raised his hands and turned around to see Jared pointing his gun at him. He looked down to see Davey, his face turned towards Otis, eyes open but lifeless. 'Sorry,' Otis said under his breath. Davey's death was down to him. It was his idea to come into the Interland. His idea to confront Zadie, to think he could persuade her to protect the source. His fault. As Zadie and the others took a further step, Otis turned and slipped through the waterfall. Shots rang out behind him but failed to connect. He ran towards the opening, knowing that the boulder would prevent him from passing through to the unnamed river, but with no other plan, he kept going.

Footsteps behind him pushed him on. He stopped at the boulder. He leaned his weight into it but only moved it a few inches, enough to make a gap but not enough to slip through. Footsteps. Otis darted across the cave, into the darkness of the dead-end in the passageway just as Jared and Simon turned the corner and piled into the space in front of the boulder.

'He's through,' one of them said.

Jared pushed the boulder out of its position so that Simon could look through. 'He's gone,' said Simon. 'Do we follow?'

'No,' said Jared. 'He's no threat out there. Step out of the way.' As Simon moved aside, Jared allowed the boulder to roll back into place, sealing the outside once more. Otis breathed relief as Simon and Jared made their way back into the Interland. He remained there in the dark corner of the cave for some time before he gathered the strength and will to leave Davey behind and push his way back out behind the boulder, back to the gateway.

36

Otis and Davey had been gone for over an hour. Samir noticed his son's discomfort and tried to distract him. 'So this is where you've been all this time?' he said.

'Not here,' said Stitch. This is just the gateway where we fought their head Reader, Marcus. Where Jay destroyed him.'

Debris still scattered the floor like the scene of an ancient battle. 'You could have got in touch,' said Samir.

Stitch looked at his dad. 'We talked about this. I left you a note,' he said.

'I read it many times,' Samir said. 'I didn't know if you were alive or dead.'

'I've already apologised,' said Stitch. 'But it's not like you even noticed if I were alive or dead before I left.'

Samir shifted in his seat. 'I know. I'm sorry for that. *Kunt fi hidad ealaa wafat walidatik…*'

'Speak English, Dad.'

'I was mourning the death of your mother. My mind was in the sky, my heart beneath the ground.'

'I was mourning too. You had your faith. What did I have?'

Samir looked at Stitch as if only realising for the first time how alone he'd been. 'I'm sorry, son.' He made to move, but his ankle was weak and he stumbled, dropping back in his seat. Stitch stood and went to him. His dad held out a hand and Stitch took it in his own. Samir leaned to kiss Stitch on both cheeks, holding him tightly by the hand. Stitch put his arms around his dad's neck and drew him into a hug. When they released, Stitch could see the glisten in Samir's eyes and felt a prickle in the corner of his own eyes, a lump in his throat.

Stitch's ears pricked. There was a second thud from behind. He released his dad's hand. There, in the opening to the passageway that carried the River Arun into the pool, was Sammy.

'Sammy,' he called out.

Stitch ran to Sammy. It felt like weeks since he'd seen him. They embraced, with Stitch's head in his chest as Sammy stood a foot taller than him. Beyond Sammy, Stitch saw Pinto helping his sister shuffle into the cave, and behind them was Alfred – *the bookseller*, as Stitch still thought of him. He noticed Alfred was struggling and moved to help him.

'Stitch,' said Alfred. 'So good to see you.' He looked past Stitch to scan the cavern for Jay. Stitch helped Alfred lower himself to sit next to Samir, who introduced himself. 'Pleased to meet you. You're Stitch's father, I've heard all about you.'

'Really?' said Samir, looking over at Stitch.

Stitch headed back to help Pinto and Toyah. 'What happened?' he asked Toyah.

'Took a bang on the head. I'll be OK.' Stitch studied

Toyah's wound on the back of her head. The damage looked minor, but she was unsteady on her feet. He told Pinto to set her down to rest.

Sammy stood with Stitch as the others settled by the fire. 'What happened?' asked Stitch.

'Zadie's destroyed the place. There were explosions. Some passageways have caved in. I don't know what she's doing but most have gone except for the few of us trapped the wrong side of the blockages.'

'How did you get out?' said Stitch.

'The Free Cave. I knew it led to the outside, just never had the guts to test it, until we had to. Wasn't sure we were going to make it to be honest. Nearly didn't.' He nodded towards Toyah and Alfred.

'How bad are they?' Stitch asked.

'Alfred's ankle I think is just a sprain. Toyah... I'm not sure. She took a heavy blow to the head and was unconscious for a while.'

'Come and rest,' said Stitch, slinging his arm around Sammy and guiding him towards the fire.

They rested as they waited for Otis and Davey. Stitch explained how Otis had insisted they go on a reconnaissance mission to get the lie of the land, figure out what they would be facing. Sammy told them that there could be others trapped in the warren of passages behind the blocked exits. He thought his dad might be in there somewhere. 'Can we break through the blocked passages?' asked Stitch.

'Those explosions brought down whole roof sections. You'd need a JCB to get through there.' Sammy thought for a moment, then added, 'I can make my way back in through the caves and bring them out.'

'No,' said Toyah from across the room. 'You're not going back in there, Sammy. It's too dangerous. There are too many side passages and crevices for you to get lost in. It all looks the same.'

'I'm not leaving my dad.'

'He might not be in there,' said Stitch. 'He might have got out with the others.'

Sammy shook his head, and Stitch knew he felt his dad's whereabouts. If anyone would know, Sammy would.

'I think Jay is close,' said Sammy. 'I can feel her. But she's weak. Is she hurt?'

Stitch shook his head. 'She's been through it, the reduction. She has a scar to show for it.' Stitch motioned the shape of Jay's scar with his finger on the side of his face. 'But she's not hurt. Same old Jay. Determined to get here to the source and put things right.'

'She thinks the source will replenish her power?'

'We all do,' said Stitch. 'It's in the legend. We just need to get her in there before the Readers get here and destroy it.'

* * *

CASSIE GUIDED the boat through the final length of tunnel, beneath the connection to the Interland, invisible above her head as they shot through and into the pool.

Jay lay back in the boat, her eyelids flickering in the twilight beneath the darkening sky. The white cliffs of the gateway looked grey in the fading light, the squawk of birds in the cliff face a reminder to Cassie of the phoenix. She believed her friend would rise, more powerful than ever. Yet she was afraid.

She stroked the side of Jay's face, turning her head so that she could look into her eyes. 'Jay? Can you hear me? What happened back there?' Cassie said, but Jay gave no sign that she heard.

Cassie pulled the boat into the side of the pool and jammed the oar into the rock, wedging the boat so that it stayed still while she dragged Jay to stand. The boat wobbled. 'Help me out here,' Cassie pleaded. Jay finally allowed some weight to be carried in her own legs, shooting Cassie a sideways glance of recognition of their predicament. Cassie got them both out of the boat and onto the rocks, where they shuffled together towards the opening to the cave that carried the Arun. Cassie hoped the others had beaten them to the gateway cavern so she could get some help with Jay. There was little chance Jay could get to the source if she couldn't stand.

'Cassie,' came the shout from Stitch as Cassie and Jay edged into the cave. Cassie breathed a sigh of relief at the sight of her friends around the fire. The relief flooded into her legs and they gave way, taking her and Jay to the floor. Sammy and Stitch reached them and propped them up, helping them over to the fire where Pinto too came and held on to Jay's hand.

'What happened?' said Sammy, taking his sister's face in his hands.

Cassie explained what had happened in the cavern on the unnamed river, and how Jay seemed to zone out, like her brain couldn't cope with the energy, or the flow of information from the environment.

'This happened before,' said Stitch. 'In the cave with the source. She seemed to pass out from the source's power.' He'd felt the strength of power himself but it channelled directly to Jay and it was as if her mind could not cope and blacked out, rebooted, and she woke a while later. Stitch said that afterwards, Jay needed complete rest. Silence and darkness. She seemed super-sensitive to stimuli. 'Let's get her out into one of those caves, keep it quiet.'

* * *

CASSIE'S HEAD ACHED, and she wondered if she was still feeling the effects of the reflection of power she experienced back at the prison. Hinton had power that she'd not experienced. It was beyond that of the Given or of the Readers. She did not know what might happen if, or when, he arrived at the Interland, what force he would bring and how they would deal with him. She was especially concerned about their ability to fight back when Jay was obviously so weak. Jay's reaction when they got to the cavern had shaken Cassie, disturbed her understanding of the nature of the powers.

She looked up as Sammy approached. He nodded to the space next to Cassie as if to ask if he could sit. 'Since when did you need permission to talk to me?' asked Cassie.

'Sorry. Wasn't sure if you wanted time alone.'

Cassie shrugged. 'It's been a hell of a few days.'

'I'm sorry about Reuben,' said Sammy. 'He was a good guy.'

'How is she?' Cassie said, nodding towards Toyah.

'I think she'll be OK.'

Just then, Otis staggered into the cavern like he was drunk. His head was lowered and his face flushed. 'Otis,' said Cassie.

'Who's Otis?' said Sammy.

'We met him on the outside, he's OK.' Cassie stood to help Otis as he stumbled towards them.

Stitch came back into the cave. 'Where's Davey?' he asked. Otis looked up at Stitch and said nothing, but he shook his head. Stitch leaned up against the wall to steady himself. 'What happened?'

Cassie helped Otis take a seat by the fire. He rubbed his

temples. 'I screwed up,' he said. 'I tried to reason with her. I tried to explain that if the Readers destroy the source then...'

'What happened to Davey?' said Stitch, impatient.

'They shot him. He pulled me out of the way and took three bullets.'

Stitch turned away and slumped to the floor.

Cassie went to him, but his eyes were far away and he looked to Cassie like he'd had enough. 'Stitch?' Cassie said.

'It's over,' said Stitch. 'Jay is out of it. What if she doesn't come around? Zadie Lawrence is out of control.' He looked at Otis and thought of Davey. 'The Readers are coming.'

PART V

37

It was over an hour later when Jay emerged from the connecting cave. Cassie and Stitch were arguing while Samir tried to calm them down. Alfred had his head lowered as he stretched his leg and cradled his swollen ankle. Cassie stood tall in Stitch's face, insisting that he needed to snap out of it, that they had to go in, whether or not Jay was with them. Sammy, Toyah and Pinto stood a few steps away from the heat of the argument.

Pinto was the first to see Jay. He leapt to his feet. 'Are you feeling better?' Pinto said, looking up at Jay with pleading eyes.

Jay nodded, smiled and looked back to the argument. 'What's going on?'

Pinto shrugged. 'They're scared. Without you, we all are.'

When Sammy saw his sister, he looked relieved and exasperated at the same time. Jay's appearance had put an end to the argument. Cassie joined them. 'Good sleep?'

'Better, thanks,' said Jay.

'Then we can stop wasting time and get up there before *they* get here.'

'They will take some time to get through the thicket. But you're right, we need to move quickly.'

Cassie turned away. Sammy put a hand on Jay's arm. 'What's the plan?'

Jay nodded towards the fire. 'Let's go through it together.'

* * *

JAY STILL HAD a wisp of hope that the Readers wouldn't make it to the Interland, and that they could persuade Zadie to end the conflict without an all-out fight. Jay still felt weak. Her power had peaked when they passed through the cavern on the unnamed river, but it had subsided. She needed to get nearer the source, and to do that, she'd have to face Zadie and the other Given that stood in her way.

Cassie led the way through to the unnamed river, Otis following close behind. Stitch nudged Jay. 'Can you freeze the river?'

Jay took a breath and closed her eyes, leaning up against the rock opening to the cave. She reached inside of herself for the buried inner energy. She shook her head. 'I'm sorry.'

Cassie put a hand on Jay's shoulder. Stitch pressed on, wading upstream, followed by Jay. At the connection, Cassie helped Otis up into the opening and one by one the five of them positioned themselves behind the main entrance, closed off by the boulder.

Jay let out a sigh. 'We ready? We do it like we said?'

Cassie nodded and leaned her shoulder into the rock. Otis helped and the boulder rolled away from the opening. On the inside, they crouched in the shadows, moving along the wall towards the water curtain ahead of them. 'The Readers aren't here. I'd feel them by now,' said Jay.

'That's good,' said Stitch. 'Let's move.'

Behind the waterfall, Zadie's presence became impossible to ignore. Jay nodded to her left and right and they walked through the water together. Wiping their eyes clear on the other side, Jay caught sight of Zadie just as she looked up. Jared and Simon reached for their weapons but Otis did as they'd planned and used his full strength to push the guns away and across the floor of the cave, out of reach. Jay and Stitch stood close to each other, their hands touching as they connected their power as best they could. Jay felt Zadie's own power rise and sensed that Stitch felt it too. He squeezed her hand and together they resisted Zadie, pushed back at her rising energy.

'Wait,' Zadie shouted, holding up her hand.

Zadie approached, four of her companions behind her. Jay noticed Jared glance over to where his gun lay across the floor. 'Jay,' said Zadie, stepping up to her. 'Good to see you again.'

'Strange way to welcome us home, Zadie,' said Jay. 'You sent me and Stitch out to get taken by the Readers. You got Reuben killed.'

Zadie shook her head. 'You kids don't get it.'

Cassie lunged for Zadie but Zadie resisted. Cassie doubled up, holding her head. She collapsed onto her knees and Jay's attempts to shield her faltered.

'We need to talk!' said Jay.

Zadie relented.

Cassie gasped for breath and Sammy helped her up.

'Why are you doing this?' said Jay.

'Oh, come on. Your little friend and I have already been through this.' She nodded at Otis. 'The Readers and the Given are united. It's no longer up to you.'

'Then you won't mind if Stitch and I head through to the source.'

Simon lunged for one of the guns. Otis reacted, moving a chair into his path. Simon tripped, landing heavily. Otis staggered, twitching and trembling. The rock walls around them began to crumble. Stones trickled down the walls to the floor, some hanging in the air as if weightless. Otis shook harder, seeming to glow from the inside.

'Otis?' said Jay. But he couldn't respond. In the confusion, Jared moved, reaching his gun and turning back on them. Jay screamed for them to move but the shot rang out before her words reached her friends. Otis went down. He looked to Jay as his legs buckled, continuing to tremble and shake as he slid towards the floor. Cassie caught him on his way down, holding him up. Another shot pinged off the cave wall next to Jay and Jared pushed forward, his gun out in front of him.

'Stop,' Zadie shouted, holding her hands up. Another shot, this time from Simon's gun. The bullet flew between Jay and Stitch. Jay flung herself to the floor where she came face to face with Otis. His eyes were closed, his breathing shallow.

'Stop.' Zadie's voice again. Silence.

Rough hands grabbed Jay by the arms, dragging her around and marching her in towards the main cavern. Simon had a gun held to Sammy and Stitch, while two others pushed Cassie behind the others.

Jay looked back at Otis. He didn't move. Zadie stood over his body, nudging his shoulder with her foot.

Jay's power seemed to fluctuate, like it was out of control, unfocused. She sensed that Otis was still alive, but the experience in the cavern of the unnamed river had shaken her confidence. It was as if the environment no longer trusted her, and it had decided to withhold the power that she needed to flow through her.

Pushed into the store room adjacent to the main cavern, Jay, Stitch, Sammy and Cassie were placed under the guard of two of Zadie's men, both armed, and both with the protection of power. Others of the Given gathered in the main cavern, some catching Jay's eye and quickly looking away. Stitch shot Jay a challenging look. She nodded. She knew what she had to do. There was only one hope left.

Jay felt a presence. Not the power of a Reader, but something more, a power signal not yet unscrambled. Hinton.

There were Readers with him, the strength of energy indicated enough to fill the gateway. She caught Stitch's eye once more. He felt it too.

38

One by one, the black boots of the Readers filed down the rope ladder and into the main cavern. One by one the Readers greeted Zadie and her companions before taking a place on a rock at the edges, waiting.

'How many are there?' Stitch said, his jaw dropping open.

Cassie paced the small space that was their temporary prison, a caged tiger ready for a fight, no matter the stacked odds. As Jay watched, she saw that the last person to descend the steps of the ladder was the only man in a suit, Hinton. In no hurry, he joined what must have been a crowd of thirty Readers edging their way around the cavern for space to stand or perch on a rock. Hinton approached Zadie, and they exchanged words that Jay couldn't hear above the background noise of marching boots. It was obvious to Jay that it wasn't the first time he and Zadie had met as they greeted each other warmly, like old friends.

'They're solid,' said Cassie, watching the interaction of Zadie and Hinton.

'All part of their plan,' Jay said, thinking back to the beginning. Before Zadie had entered the Interland, she'd been taken by the State, held in captivity for months before escaping to the Interland. 'They got to Zadie when she was inside, in rehabilitation.'

'But she's not a Reader. Her power comes from the source,' said Stitch. 'She's one of the Given.'

'She has the scar,' said Cassie. 'Maybe she *is* a Reader?'

'No,' said Jay. 'She's just forgotten how to be. She's been twisted by this man.' Jay looked at her wrist. Her marking was no more than an indecipherable smudge, little more than had appeared back at the hill forts. Jay looked over at Stitch and saw him check his own wrist, the dark letter "C" still as it had always been, now waiting for Jay's connection that was proving evasive.

'The fact that the Readers could get in here,' said Stitch, 'tells us that me and Jay are not properly connected. It's not enough that we're here in the Interland, we need to get to the source. We need to connect if we stand any chance. They can't remain here if the eight-C and the C are connected.'

'We need to get through the cavern, past them,' said Jay. She turned to Sammy. 'Dad must be through there,' she said, nodding towards the blockage of the rock tunnel, but they had no way to get through to reach Ben, Matchstick, or anyone else that might be trapped behind the blockages and could help.

A shout came up over the sound of the crowd of Readers. Zadie called for quiet and the faces of the Given and Readers together turned to look towards Zadie and Hinton, elevated on Zadie's platform she used for all her speeches in the Interland.

'We are finally united,' she said. A muffled cheer

emanated from the Readers and the Given that stood at Zadie's feet. 'We must now safeguard the source for future generations of the Given and Readers. Together!' The crowd remained quiet, some looks of confusion between the Readers. Jay watched their faces and realised that, as she had known, the Readers had no intention of protecting the source. Zadie continued, 'We must secure the sanctity of the source as a place of pilgrimage.'

Stitch looked at Jay. 'She has no idea,' he said.

Zadie brimmed with energy, building to a punchline. 'We will ensure that the magic of the Interland is protected, not as a subterranean prison that hides the Given from society, but as a place to visit, an epicentre and symbol of peace.' She thrust her fist into the air to an unenthusiastic mumbling in the crowd.

'Thank you,' said Hinton, taking a place on the podium next to Zadie. 'And listen,' he said, silencing the crowd. 'Zadie here will be our first in command, as a Reader, she will be the State's leader of all Readers.'

'You misunderstand,' said Zadie to Hinton, just loud enough that Jay could hear. 'I am part of the Given. *We* are the Given.' She cast her arm across the crowd. 'We will remain the Given, and we will work together for the benefit of society. We can rebuild this country as an integrated force, Given and Reader together.'

Hinton smiled and placed an arm around Zadie. He turned to the crowd. 'You think the Given can remain in a new society?' People muttered. 'The time of the Given has run its course.' He turned back to Zadie, his arm remaining around her neck and his smile broadening. 'Thanks to Zadie, we have access to the source. There is no connected power to repel the Readers from this place.' He looked directly to where Jay and the others stood under guard at the back. 'And we cannot let that power become re-established. This is our window of opportunity to end this battle.'

Jay felt the tension rising in the great cavern, but the odds were stacked against any resistance that Zadie and the Given might present. The Readers were too powerful and there were too many of them. Zadie stood virtually alone against the full power of the Readers, unprotected by the 8C. She had delivered Hinton his plan with absolutely no resistance.

A white glow twinkled in the distance. It was almost unnoticeable, a slight mist with a sparkle as it drew nearer.

In the cavern, Zadie seemed to shrink in stature up on the podium. But her expression, and the energy that Jay felt coming from her, showed no signs that she was about to give up her power, or allow the source to be destroyed by the Readers. A shot rang out through the cavern and Jared jumped up next to Zadie.

Zadie lashed out at Hinton, shoving him and sending him into the crowd. A scuffle at Zadie's feet sent Jared back into the crowd. He dropped his gun. Hinton drifted towards the back of the cave, away from the fighting, a smile fixed on his face as if his job was done. The Given were outnumbered, but they fought hard, Zadie using her power to gain any advantage.

Cassie jiggled on her feet, pacing the store room, occasionally stopping to see what was happening in the fight. Jay peered through the entrance to the cavern as a wave of energy seemed to flow above the heads of the Readers. A swirling dust gathered. 'Otis?' said Stitch.

Jay shook her head. 'No. If he's alive, he's not strong enough.' As they watched, more dust gathered, with stones and other debris as if controlled by a level 5. 'It's Pinto,' she said. 'I can feel him. He's working the energy from the Gateway.'

'Alf was right,' said Cassie. 'He's like Otis.' The dust and stones swirled around the heads of the Readers, creating confusion and balancing the odds a little.

The guards outside the storeroom had been distracted by the chaos. Cassie took the opportunity and launched herself into an attack on the two guards. They both hit the floor, and Cassie threw herself into the throng. Jay watched, wide-eyed, as Cassie used her well-honed martial arts skills to take down Reader after Reader. Jay turned to see that the white glow at the passageway had intensified, a white mist reaching towards the entrance to the storeroom in which she was held. Sammy put a hand on Jay's shoulder. 'Go,' he said, nodding towards the mist. 'Just hurry.' He turned and piled into the crowd behind Cassie.

Stitch grabbed Jay's arm, and they stepped out of the store cavern concealed by the white mist that was now leaking through to the main cavern. They picked up speed, striding in the direction of the source. Before they left the main cavern, someone stepped out to block their path. Hinton stood before them. 'That's not going to happen,' he said. Stitch lifted a hand to push him aside but was stopped by the force of the Readers, not coming from this suited man but channelled from the surrounding Readers.

'Stop,' Jay said, and Hinton released Stitch from his agony. Jay turned to see that Cassie and Sammy were stood with Jared and Simon, the men that had killed Otis, and probably Davey. Cassie fought hard. Sammy was knocked to the floor as Jay looked on. 'That's enough,' said Jay.

She looked at the man, and his gaze drifted from Jay to something behind her in the distance. She turned. Someone was coming down the ladder through the opening in the roof. Then another, a stream of people. The fighting below seemed to freeze as they all looked up into the roof. 'It's Marcus,' whispered Jay as Stitch dragged himself back to stand.

'Marcus?' said Hinton. Streams of people came down from the surface and Marcus approached Jay, Stitch and Hinton. The Readers turned to observe the interaction, unsure of the intentions of the new crowd as reinforcements or the enemy. 'Marcus,' said Hinton. 'It's been some time.' Hinton looked at Jay, 'Marcus was my first,' he said, pride in his voice. 'I thought you were dead.'

Marcus turned his head so that Hinton could see his two parallel scars. 'A battle scar thanks to this young lady, I gather?' said Hinton. Marcus nodded. 'So you've come to witness the end of the source? To join in our finest hour as Readers?'

Marcus nodded again and turned to Jay. He winked, then turned round and knocked Hinton off his feet. No sooner had the man hit the floor, Marcus went down in pain as Hinton brought the power of the Readers down on him. The fighting in the cavern resumed. 'Go,' Marcus said between gritted teeth as he forced himself to his feet again. Marcus had rallied hidden Given in support of his mission to help Jay, to save the source and the Interland, and now they all joined the fray.

Stitch grabbed Jay as she stared at Marcus, the Given and the throng of people fighting, this time with more balanced sides. Hinton raised himself from the floor and Marcus lashed out at him again, grimacing at the pain in his own head but managing to get the better of the man. Jay allowed Stitch to pull her down the passageway through an intensifying glow of white mist. 'What is this?' said Jay as she ran alongside Stitch.

'I think we know what this is,' Stitch shouted with excitement. 'This is the other Interlands connecting.'

Jay recalled the man, the islands, and the black tendrils of darkness surrounding them, suffocating the land. As they reached the connection to the source, they stopped. The white glow was at its most intense, at the blocked connection to the rest of the Interland. The rock mass seemed to liquify inside the mist, flowing like water. 'What...' said Jay, staring.

'No time,' said Stitch, pressing on down into the cavern of the source.

HINTON TURNED TO MARCUS, tired of his attempts to keep him down. He drew on the power of the Readers in the cavern, over thirty of them with a combined energy level that could not be deflected by any of the Given, however many tried to combine. He pierced Marcus's mind with the full force of the Readers' power. Marcus crumpled before him, his face in the dust at the man's feet. He pushed harder, relentlessly digging into Marcus's weak mind, his already damaged defences. Marcus was weaker than he'd thought. The reduction and transformation back to the Given had taken him from one of the strongest that Hinton had ever created, to a Given with little means of defence. He pushed harder.

Another of the Given approached, but immediately fell to the floor under Hinton's energy. Marcus's breathing wheezed as he was crushed into the floor as if by a heavy rockfall. Hinton crouched, not letting up the channelling of power for a second but increasing the digging as Marcus's defences crumpled. Until Marcus stopped breathing. He turned over to lie on his back as he released his final breath. The marking on his wrist was a mass of blood, steaming as if it had been burned off. The two scars on the side of his face had merged to a mass of red. His eyes, still open, communicated a defiance with no substance.

Marcus was dead. Hinton stood and turned towards the passageway to the source where Jay and Stitch had disappeared in the hope of protecting it. 'You're too late,' Hinton said aloud as he moved into the mist.

39

Cassie looked over the heads of the crowd to see Hinton slip away through the passageway after Jay and Stitch, a gaggle of Readers following him like a cloak flowing in his slipstream. She took a blow to the head, and as she felt the blood dripping down her face, she wondered how much more she could take. She swept the legs away from the Reader in front of her, then disabled him with a single punch to the underside of his nose. She looked around for Sammy. She'd had no sight of him for some minutes.

With Marcus's reinforcements, there were as many of the Given as there were Readers, but Cassie could see that the Readers remained stronger, both in their power and their physical strength. They used their power to confuse and disorientate, then their fighting ability to take the Given down. Many had fallen unconscious or worse. Cassie continued to fight like it was the last fight on earth. None of these Readers would get the better of her.

She moved towards the exit, closer to where Jay would need her help. Two Readers stepped in front of her and she wasn't sure if she could lift her arms to fight, she was so exhausted. She steadied herself and kicked out, taking one of them down with a kick to the face, then the other with a leg-sweep. Two more appeared, one landing a heavy blow to Cassie's head. She wobbled, spinning, but she didn't go down, not until a third Reader clumped her on the head from behind. The last thing she saw was the black boot of a Reader in the dust in front of her eyes. Then it moved, swung backwards and came rushing towards her face.

40

J ay stumbled down the rock steps towards the source, her head pounding with pain and confusion. She couldn't get a handle on her power. The energy inside her felt bigger than her. She was not worthy of it, had no sense of control over it. She was afraid of it.

Footsteps behind them. 'Readers,' said Stitch.

Jay sensed it was not just Readers, but also Hinton. She communicated this to Stitch without words. They picked up their pace, but Jay already felt the influence of the man behind them. He was pushing, prodding and delving into Jay's mind. Her head spun and Stitch turned to look at her, instinctively taking her arm and guiding her down the final few steps into the darkness of the lowest level of the Interland. Jay could do nothing but slump onto the floor as Stitch moved to light a candle to provide just enough light to get to the three streams of water – the source.

He leaned to help Jay up, dragging her by the elbow. 'Come on,' he shouted above the noise coming from above. 'It's time. You can do this. You *have* to do this.'

Jay stood and nodded. They faced each other and locked eyes and braced for what they knew was coming. Then came the energy of the Readers, like a tsunami of dark power flooding down the stairs. Stitch went down, floored by the power of the Readers channelled by Hinton. Jay stood firm, the power growing in her. Hinton appeared and pushed her off her feet without a single touch.

He ignored Stitch and bore down on Jay. 'No more, Jay. This is it. This is enough. Let it go.' He pierced her mind, pushing and digging. Jay could feel his determination, the hate and anger inside him. She could feel her own mind giving way, moving as if controlled by him. Out of the corner of her eye she saw Readers behind him, entering the cavern one by one. As each crossed the threshold, she felt the pain sharpen, a more powerful infiltration. They kept coming. Jay closed her eyes, unable to see for the darkness surrounding her. She concentrated her effort on shielding the attack, biding her time.

Jay was barely conscious when Hinton stopped. Her eyelids were too heavy to open. She heard their words as they talked of the source. 'Is this it?' came the unimpressed voice of one of the Readers. Jay opened an eye to see the man and two of the Readers leaning over the source above Jay's head.

The man put his fingers into the water and Jay wondered whether this would connect him with the power. 'Nothing,' he said. Jay's mind continued to spin. She was unable to open her other eye for fear of falling into the earth. Hinton grunted with derision as he sloshed his fingers around in the water. He cupped his hands and drank, smacking his lips and laughing with the Readers. 'Nothing,' Hinton said again, then swished some water around in his mouth before spitting it out into the flow from above.

Stitch moved, catching Jay's eye. He was a few feet from her, his movement slow and painful. Hinton splashed in the source once more and water fell to the ground between Jay and Stitch. Stitch leaned to touch the water, wetting his fingers and rubbing the water into their tips.

He reached for Jay and she opened out her hand to receive his. He wet her fingers with his own and a spark passed between them, up into Jay's mind, settling her racing thoughts, the pounding in her head subsiding.

She opened her other eye and looked directly at Stitch. She felt his heartbeat. It was weak. He closed his eyes.

Jay reached for the spilled water from the source, took it onto her fingers, and reached out to Stitch. Gently, she brushed the water from the source onto Stitch's lips. She felt the tingle as her connection with Stitch and with the source pushed energy through their bodies.

Again, Jay dipped her fingers into the pool beside her as Hinton and the Readers laughed above their heads. She brushed more onto Stitch's lips and this time he opened his eyes and they sparkled with light.

Jay clenched her teeth in determination, opening her mind and body to the flow of energy, no longer a thought for the danger the power of the connection might bring.

This time, she reciprocated the power. She channelled the energy through her body and back to Stitch.

Her sleeve was pushed up her arm, and she looked down at it, the number eight clear and full, the letter "C" discernible once more. She turned her arm to show Stitch. He smiled and shifted his weight on his shoulder so that he could rest on his hand. He cast his eyes up to the Readers and nodded to Jay.

Jay saw that Hinton had stepped back from the edge of

the pool where the three streams of water flowed. Stitch stood and immediately the Readers turned on him. Jay jumped up to stand with him and together they thrust their hands into the water.

Hinton turned, fear and surprise on his face. Their power was evident, and he knew immediately this was his last chance. He threw everything he had at Jay and Stitch. As they reached for each other to make the connection, their bodies were thrown apart. Their hands remained connected to the pool of the source, but they couldn't reach each other to connect the circle.

Hinton pushed with all the power of the Readers in the room. Jay and Stitch swayed and bucked as they held their hands in the water and reached for each other.

A swirling mist, a white glow, seeped towards them from the passageway.

Jay looked over to Stitch, whose face was contorted in pain. She willed him to look at her and he slowly turned his eyes towards her. Mist swirled between them and Jay blocked out the vision of Hinton, the anger and determination in his face to end her and Stitch. She focused only on Stitch, and on opening to the energy of the source. As his eyes drifted away from her, she screamed his name, pulling him back.

The mist thickened and Jay reached out her hand, but Stitch was too far away.

The mist swirled around Stitch's arm and seemed to help him fight against the power of the Readers and raise his arm towards Jay. Their fingers now just inches apart, the white energy passed between them, the mist wrapping its tendrils around each of their wrists and pulling their hands together.

They touched.

The white glow intensified and exploded throughout the room. The Readers who filled the room writhed in pain as their energy soaked into the walls and their bodies became entwined in the stretching roots, vines and wisps of the mist in the cavern.

Hinton laughed. 'This power does nothing to me, I am immune.'

As the words drifted from him, the connection that Stitch and Jay had made with the earth, and the piercing white glow combined, pushing energy out through every cell in Jay's body.

As she shook with the power, the floor vibrated and Jay's vision blurred once more as a figure appeared in the mist – the man from the lake. A white glow emanated from him, drifting so that its epicentre floated between Jay and Stitch, surrounding them and joining with the source.

The power of the Interland exploded through the room. Hinton released a guttural scream as his physical form dissolved into the mist, his body melting into the rocks of the cavern and seeping into the walls like crude oil slipping away through the cracks.

The man from the lake disappeared but the white light remained, growing in its intensity then shooting out through the opening and up the steps towards the main cavern, destroying every Reader in its path. The connection of the level 8C and her connected C became whole.

The Interland was once again protected.

* * *

JAY OPENED HER EYES, spitting out the dust in her mouth and pushing herself up to sit. Stitch woke and sat up, rubbing his head. The white light that surrounded them began to dissipate and Jay recognised where they were. Water lapped the shore near her feet, and behind Stitch was the tree that stretched high into the sky in the middle of the island.

They were back on the island in the lake. The mist cleared. Jay saw the outline of the man, the other 8C, come into view. He had waded into the water up to his waist and he waved her and Stitch to come join him. Jay looked down into the water, where the black swirls of darkness had before wrapped around Stitch, burning his skin. The water was clear. The swirls in the water carried fish and reeds. Jay led the way and Stitch followed. They got to the man when the water had reached their waists. He held out a hand to each of Jay and Stitch. 'Thank you,' he said.

Jay smiled. 'We couldn't have done it without you.'

'I wasn't there. Not as such. Only in your mind. In your connected power I was there.'

Jay turned to Stitch. Tears leaked down his face, and Jay put a hand on his shoulder. 'It's over, Stitch.'

The man turned his gaze to the other islands, far across the lake. Jay and Stitch followed the direction of his gaze. The blackened islands seemed darker, not lighter from what Jay could see. 'Why...' Jay started.

'The Readers,' said the man. 'Not your Readers, other Readers. When I saw you last, there were three islands down and two under threat, yours being one of those under threat. Now there are four islands down, but thanks to your work, this island,' he nodded behind Jay and Stitch, 'has been released.'

Jay looked on. Swirls of darkness touched at the edges of a fifth island, the island that was closest to this man's. 'The darkness is drawing closer?'

He nodded. 'Yes. And to fight it, we'll need your help.'

'How?'

'I'll show you. There is time, not much, but some. And you both need to rest.' Jay looked over to where the islands appeared to be darkening by the minute. Stitch looked to Jay, and they knew that they would have no choice.

They had a mission.

As Jay and Stitch clambered back up the steps from the deep cavern that held the source, Jay felt the energy flowing through her bones. Sparks filled the air between her and Stitch, like static electricity. She felt as strong as she'd ever been.

'Jay,' came a shout from the darkness in the tunnel at the top of the steps. Jay recognised the voice of her father. He came into the light, Matchstick by his side, and she allowed herself to melt into her dad's embrace, the sparks of her power surrounding them both. Beyond him and Matchstick, a group of the Given emerged from behind a mass of rocks and stones that had previously blocked the passageway.

'What happened?' said Jay, releasing her dad and nodding towards the opening in the rockfall.

'A flow of water, mist or something came from through the rocks and washed out the blockage. We've been trapped in there for days. There's no other way out.' Jay smiled at the knowledge that Sammy had found a way through and then led Alfred, Toyah and Pinto to freedom.

Ben looked beyond Jay to see Stitch leaning up against the rocks. 'What happened to you? Where's Sammy?'

Jay turned towards the main cavern, momentarily concerned for Cassie and Sammy. She sensed they were safe. The Readers had gone.

The main cavern looked like it had been hit by an earthquake. Debris lay all around – bits of the dining table, chairs. The picture of Sasha Colden had been knocked from the wall and lay on the floor. Cassie and Sammy leaned up against the rocks at the edge of the cave. Their eyes were closed as they rested, and Cassie had her head on Sammy's shoulder. Jay breathed a sigh of relief.

Some of the Given hadn't made it. Jay saw at least three dead, and others sporting wounds being patched by others. A movement in the distance, up near the waterfall, caught Jay's eye, and she strained to see four figures emerge through the water and head towards them.

Alfred and Samir came into view first, Samir gaping. His first impression of the Interland was one of total devastation. Toyah and Pinto followed. Pinto ran ahead, overtaking Alfred and Samir to shoot through to the cavern. 'Jay,' he shouted.

Jay met him halfway, and he jumped up to embrace her. 'We were worried. The noises were so loud, we thought the whole place had been destroyed. Are the Readers gone?'

Jay nodded, lowering Pinto to the floor. 'They've gone.' Jay crouched down with Pinto. 'Was that you? Earlier? Did you use power?'

Pinto nodded, a grin widening. 'Did it work?'

Jay smiled at him. 'You bet it did. You helped distract the guards that held us. It was chaos in here. I reckon Alf here was right about you.'

'Is Otis OK?' Pinto asked, looking past Jay. Cassie had moved over to tend to Otis, his shirt covered in blood from a wound in his shoulder.

Jay and Pinto rushed over to them, and Jay crouched. 'Hey, crazy man,' she said. 'What happened? You totally spun out.'

Otis looked up and smiled. 'Something in the power sent me a little mad for a while back there. I lost control. Then I froze.'

'Are you OK?'

'I'll live,' he said.

Toyah joined them. Jay placed a hand on her arm. 'How's your head?'

'I'll live,' she replied, then looked beyond Jay to see Sammy as he rose from the floor. He and Toyah met, and he pulled her into a hug. Jay watched as Toyah held her brother tight, closing her eyes. Sammy looked at Jay over Toyah's shoulder, then over to Cassie who stood to greet Alfred and Samir. Jay leaned to pick up the picture of Sasha Colden. She pushed the wooden frame back into place and offered it up to the wall. It hung on a protruding piece of rock and Jay straightened it. She turned away and saw her dad pulling a cover over Zadie Lawrence. She glimpsed her lifeless eyes, staring up at Ben.

One by one, they climbed out of the Interland through the opening in the roof. Jay climbed the rope ladder behind Alfred, helping to guide his feet into the right places as he climbed. Cassie helped Otis as he struggled with his shoulder.

At the surface, with few words, they climbed to the crest of the hill, the peak that could be seen from where the river Arun flowed into the floodplain. Jay stood at the high point and looked down through the trees where she saw the river. Stitch joined her. 'The Arun?' he said.

'Yes,' said Jay. 'And see there,' she pointed. 'That's the Rother coming in. Can't see the unnamed river from here.'

'That one doesn't surface until its way beyond those hills.' Stitch nodded into the distance. They looked over at Cassie, stood alone on a rock, her braids sticking out at angles they'd not seen before. She kicked at the dirt, sending dust into the wind. She hugged her arms.

Jay imagined Reuben standing next to her. 'She's been through it these last few days. She's going to need some looking after,' she said.

Stitch nodded towards Sammy and Toyah as they looked out over the north ridge, holding hands. They watched as Sammy glanced over to Cassie and it seemed for a moment that he'd head over to join her, but then changed his mind. Ben was with Otis. They wandered up to join Sammy and Toyah, Ben pulling his son away from Toyah for a moment as he slung an arm around his shoulder.

Alfred and Samir had found a rock to rest on at the front of the ridge, looking over the hills of the Downs. Pinto ran to them and Toyah called for him to be careful. Pinto planted himself between Alfred and Samir, pointing them towards the north and across the fields. Jay heard him describe the route that he and Toyah had taken to get to the Interland.

'How do you remember back that far?' said Alfred, ruffling Pinto's hair.

'I'll never forget,' Pinto said in a serious tone, holding Alfred's gaze for a moment.

Alfred pulled him in to hug. 'I know, little one. I know.'

Jay looked further into the distance and imagined the other Interlands, under attack, in danger of being overtaken by the darkness. She felt Stitch's hand drift close to hers and without looking at him she twined her fingers through his. He clutched her hand tightly, and together they stared out across the hills and river valley, towards the distant sea.

End of Book #2

THANK YOU!

I hope you enjoyed my second book in the Interland series.

Reviews are really important for new authors like me. If you can spare a minute to leave a short review on your preferred store, just a sentence or two, then I'd be very grateful - Thanks!

If you've not joined my Reader Club, where you can keep up to date on forthcoming publications, news and freebies to go with the INTERLAND series - including a free eBook prequel called *The Reader*, an insight to Marcus and his background - then please join by visiting my website -

www.garyclarkauthor.co.uk

ABOUT THE AUTHOR

Gary graduated from the University of Surrey in the UK with a degree in Engineering, embarking on a career that has taken him all over the world from the Far East to the Americas. He is a graduate of the Faber Academy and Curtis Brown creative writing programmes. Now a father of three, he has settled with his family close to where he grew up on the edge of the South Downs in Sussex, where he indulges his love of books, and passion for writing.

I'd love to hear from you so feel free to contact me on the email address below - let me know what you thought of the book. And look out for Book #3 - *The Dark*.

gary@garyclarkauthor.co.uk

Or visit my website

www.garyclarkauthor.co.uk

First published 2021 GCL Books.

www.garyclarkauthor.co.uk

Paperback ISBN 978 1 8384010 1 6